Halfway to Creepy

(A Collection of Bizarre Short Stories)

by

Anthony Mays

This book is a work of fiction. All names, characters, places, dialogue, and incidents either are the product of the author's imagination or are used fictitiously, and any resemblance to actual persons, living or dead, businesses, companies, events, or locales is entirely coincidental.

Halfway to Creepy by Anthony Mays. Copyright © 2016 by Anthony Mays

All rights reserved. No part of this work may be reproduced, scanned, or distributed in any printed or electronic form without permission.

Book cover photo courtesy of: Sheri Pennock

ISBN-13: 978-1534734036 (CreateSpace-Assigned)
ISBN-10: 1534734031

Dedication

This collection is dedicated to all those fans of horror and psychological thrillers. A special thank you goes to my grandson, Bram, who introduced me to the creepy closet and showed me that creepy can be fun.

Author Forward

Let me first thank you for selecting my book.

This book is a collection of bizarre, short stories that stem from my childhood memories of watching too many Alfred Hitchcock movies and Twilight Zone episodes. You may find there is a certain familiarity about them from your own experiences. There seems to be little distinction between the definitions of horror and creepy, but I believe horror is more imagery, whereas, creepy is more imagination. I also classify these stories as psychological thrillers, which often overlaps with the elements of mystery and horror. What I hope I achieved with these stories was to stimulate your imagination sufficiently to allow your mind to fill in those blank areas where I purposefully did not detail a scene or conclusion.

I wrote these stories between the writings of my novels as a way to keep my skills fresh. If you find that you enjoyed any of these stories, I invite you to try one of my thriller novels.

Anthony Mays

Table of Contents

Copyright	ii
Dedication	iii
Author Forward	iv
Table of Contents	v
White Knuckles	1
Halfway to an Illusion – Man in the Mirror	7
Last Magic Act	34
Halfway to a Prophesy – The Stone	46
Joy	68
Gypsies	78
Halfway to May 18th	98
Norse Coffer	107
Author's Note	130
About the Author	131

White Knuckles

Sam was staring through the windshield of his black 2009 Audi, but the rain and darkness prevented him from seeing anything more than a few high bushes outside his vehicle. His heart was pounding inside his chest. His fingers gripped the steering wheel so tightly that his knuckles were white. He couldn't believe how close he had just come to dying.

Sam was familiar with that stretch of road; he took it every day to work. The winding road ran along a tree and shrub lined ridge, which paralleled a remote valley floor at least one hundred feet below. From the road to the edge of the embankment was only about forty feet, and Sam knew he must have travelled almost every bit of that distance.

He sat there trembling, speculating as to the cause of his skidding off the road. He could blame it on any number of things, the pounding rain, the darkness, the bends in the road, or even the condition of his vehicle. But he quickly realized that he was the cause of his own situation. He had been speeding in an area that was well marked with road signs reading: SLOW Road Curves Ahead CAUTION. He was speeding because he was angry. The fact was, he had been angry all day.

His anger had begun early that morning, when he tripped over a toy that his four-year-old boy had left at the bottom of the steps. He remembered yelling profusely at his son. *Why can't you ever keep your toys where they belong? I'm sick and tired of you leaving them everywhere. You don't deserve to have any of them.* He recalled picking up the toy and tossing it across the room, and then watching as his son cried hard and ran to his mother.

At the breakfast table, he had argued with his wife about her mother's upcoming weekend visit. He thought she was visiting too often and her visits interfered with him enjoying his own home during his free time.

He had shouted, "I don't like it that your mother comes to visit every other weekend. I feel I don't have any privacy. Can't we just be by ourselves for a little while?"

His wife quarreled back, pointing out that her mother was only trying to do them a favor by helping with their son so they could find some time to relax.

"After all," she had cried, "while you are away all day, all I do is take care of our son and this household. Maybe *I* need some time to *myself*."

He fought back declaring that he was out making a living so they all could have the things they needed and a roof over their heads. "It's not as though I'm out having fun all day," he'd added.

Later that morning, he and a co-worker got into a fight about a client's account. Sam believed that the other employee was trying to steal the client away from him. "This is my account," he'd grumbled. "I worked hard to bring this client into the company, and now you're trying to pilfer the account?"

Sam had blocked out the co-worker's explanation that their supervisor had thrown the account on his desk the previous afternoon, with a note to take action.

They spent the rest of the day trying to ignore each other, without much success. Emotions ran high on both sides.

When Sam attended a meeting that afternoon, he learned that his boss needed him to work late on a new marketing campaign. He had been planning to arrive home early to watch the season opener of his favorite television show. He had forgotten to set up a recording of the show, and knew his wife wouldn't be able to figure out the remote control to do it for him.

"Why me? Why today of all days?" He had said aloud to the gathered group; his boss clearly not amused by his outburst.

When he completed his work and was able to leave for the evening, he arrived at his car only to find a flat tire. To make matters worse, rain started to fall making changing the tire even more unpleasant. Sam spent the better part of an hour working on the spare tire, while his clothes stuck to him, soaked from the rain.

Finally, he was able to drive home - but he wondered if he had sufficiently tightened all the lug nuts on the spare tire. "There's no way I'm getting out in this weather again," he spoke aloud to himself. "Not if my life depended on it."

He stepped on the pedal, not letting the slick road ahead be a deterrent to making up for lost time.

But now, here he was, at the edge of a cliff, listening to the windshield wipers swish from side to side. The car's engine stalled, but the wipers and the car lights continued to run off battery power. He counted his blessings that he had not gone over the edge and careened down the one-hundred-foot embankment. His close call with death led him to vow that, when he got home, he would make things right with his son and wife.

"I was such a jerk to them today!" He admitted. "And when I return to work tomorrow, I owe a ton of apologies to everyone."

Suddenly, Sam heard sirens approaching his location and was relieved that emergency vehicles would soon arrive to help him out of his situation. He tried to get out of the vehicle to meet them, but he couldn't move. He couldn't move his arms or legs and wondered what had happened that could have caused his body parts to shut down. He could only sit and wait for the assistance that was coming closer to him.

He first saw a police officer walk to the front of his car and look into the canyon below.

Sam began to yell at him to come and help him get out of the Audi.

Then several firemen approached, taking up positions next to the police officer with all of them looking over the edge of the cliff.

He couldn't believe that they were ignoring him, and he screamed at the top of his lungs, "*Hey get me out of this vehicle. I can't move! What the hell is so is so important down there that you can ignore me? What's wrong with you people? Please, I need your help!*"

With the rain still falling, it was hard for him to hear what they were saying. He strained to listen to their conversation, and then froze in fear. He was able to make out some words the police officer relayed to the firemen. The officer had told them that another driver thought he saw a black Audi go off the road and over the embankment.

"This can't be happening!" Sam shrieked. "I'm here! Right behind you. Turn around and look at me!"

Suddenly, he could move and he quickly got out of the vehicle and ran over to where the men were standing. He looked in the direction the officer pointed to and saw distant lights on a vehicle that was upside down near the bottom of the valley.

He heard the officer say, "Whoever was in that vehicle didn't make it. I'm going to call in and let them know this won't be a rescue operation. We'll be needing a recovery team instead."

A short distance from where they were standing, Sam saw a familiar tire rolled onto its side in the thick underbrush. The image struck him with horror. He finally understood that he was no longer with the living, and was taking his last look at how his miserable day ended.

END

HALFWAY TO AN ILLUSION – MAN IN THE MIRROR

No Denying It...

Sebastian sat on the well-worn, Windsor chair staring into the mirror with only his reflection gazing back. His mind could not fathom the hideous, monstrous crimes he was recently accused of committing, yet the evidence was undeniable.

"That the mirror you told us about?" asked a figure moving behind him, breaking into his thoughts.

"Yes... this is where I would come and sit when I felt remorse or guilt." Mechanically, the words escaped his lips, but Sebastian could not believe he was the one saying them as he continued his stare. "I am not a bad person."

"Alright Mr. Kimball, I am confident this room will be evidence for your defense. At least it should keep you from getting a death sentence."

The lawyer then nodded to the officer standing next to his client suggesting that was all they needed, and he could return him to lockup.

The officer leaned over to assist his prisoner out of the chair, and Sebastian stood, automatically turning his back and putting his hands behind him to receive the handcuffs.

The mirror leaned against the attic wall. It was a large Victorian pane of glass trimmed by thick, carved, mahogany wood. It was easily four-foot wide and over six-feet tall. Parts of the glass were cloudy, suggesting it was not new. An abundant amount of dust had collected in the crevices of the carving and along the flat edges.

"I'm going to take a few photos before any of this stuff gets moved. Is this the way the room always looked when you came here?" asked his lawyer, before he was escorted off.

A sullen nod was all Sebastian could muster as he blankly took a last look into the mirror at his pathetic image.

The flash of the camera reflected off the glass, temporarily blinding him and forcing him to close his eyes. While the bright light lingered behind his eyelids, he tried to understand how he had arrived at being charged with multiple murders.

His mind flashed back to Saint Patrick's Day three months ago, when Sebastian finally acquired the nerve to confront his demons. He vividly recalled the cheap window displays of leprechauns, four-leaf clovers, and pots of gold as he passed by them on the way to Dr. Randolph Lockwood's office. He remembered, as he entered the stairwell to the Doctor's office on the third floor of a three-story building, a tacky sign taped on the entrance door of the bar on the first floor. It read: *Erin Go Brah! Join us for laughter and fun tonight, because today, everybody is Irish. Green beer - $1.* Two things immediately struck him. Firstly, he thought Brah was misspelled, leaving out a 'g'; and, secondly, the name of the bar was *Daisy's Place*.

He waited in a small outer office wondering how the Doctor would know he had arrived. There was no receptionist. Two black leather chairs with a tiered table between them was all that welcomed him. An antique brass lamp sat on top of the table, and tattered magazines were spread across the second shelf. The eyes of a giant, green frog on the cover of a *National Geographic* magazine never seemed to leave him. He looked at the two pictures hanging on the opposite wall. One was a fall scene of hills and trees as one might see in a New England setting. The other was a poster of a book cover that read: *The Interpretation of*

Dreams by Sigmund Freud. Both looked as if they had come from somebody's attic.

After a few minutes, the door to an office opened and out stepped a bearded man wearing a white pin-striped shirt beneath a sleeveless, navy-blue sweater and black cuffed pants.

"Mr. Kimball, I'm Dr. Lockwood," he said, extending his hand in greeting. "You may come in now."

He waved a hand toward the door.

The office inside was just as stark as outside. An oak desk sat in a corner of the room with the only window behind it. Two identical wooden chairs on rollers were positioned front and back of the desk. A leather couch was situated nearby with the head facing away from the desk and toward the door. The wall left of the desk held several certificates of the Doctor's credentials and, off to the side, was a filing cabinet. The other walls each had cheap pictures hanging on them, similar to the waiting area.

Both men sat opposite each other on the wooden chairs.

"So Mr. Kimball, what brings you here?" the Doctor asked in a soft voice, his hands folded on his desk.

"I'm not sure exactly," Sebastian hesitated. "Sometimes I have an overwhelming feeling that I've done something horrible. I know I haven't, but I can't get things out of my mind. It's affecting my sleep, and I felt it was time to talk about it with a professional."

The Doctor opened a legal-size folder on his desk, grabbed a pen, and started taking notes. "What is it you feel you've done?"

Sebastian fidgeted in his chair – it squeaked as he moved. "Do you remember the fire at City Hall two years ago?" It was a rhetorical question and he didn't wait for an answer before continuing. "I used to work in the City Clerk's office and... well, I've been tormenting myself that I started the fire. I'm sure I didn't ... I mean I know I didn't do it, but *I believe* I did. It's not so much the fire itself, but thinking about that older woman who died from smoke inhalation has me feeling guilty, as though I caused her death."

"Is that when you believe all this started?"

The chair squeaked some more. "No. When I was about fourteen, I had a similar experience when my mother broke her leg falling on the stairs. I believed that I had pushed her, but at the time of the incident I was on the school bus. And again, when I was twenty, I believed I had caused an automobile accident that left a fellow university student paralyzed. I haven't had any thoughts like that for the past thirty years. That is, until recently."

"I see," said Dr. Lockwood, scribbling on his pad. "There definitely seems to be a pattern from childhood, but it may take a few sessions to get to the root of it."

He downed his pen, refolded his hands, and looked Sebastian in the eyes. "I know you want answers right away," he said. "Everybody does. But when it comes to the mind, sorting out the problem can be tricky. However, I think you came to the right place. I have worked with others who have had similar issues as you described and, together, we were able to lessen their fears."

Feeling encouraged, Sebastian asked, "I know this was just a preliminary visit, but when do you think we can begin regular sessions?"

The Doctor thumbed through a desk calendar, then replied, "I can start you next week and schedule weekly meetings on Thursdays at four o'clock. Would that be a good time for you?"

"Yes. I'm only working part-time now and my afternoons are free. Thank you for seeing me Dr. Lockwood. I'm looking forward to your help."

The two men shook hands, and then the Doctor escorted Sebastian to the main door and Sebastian departed the office.

Dr. Lockwood returned to his office and tore off the notes he had made on his legal pad. He went over to the filing cabinet and pulled a blank folder from the second drawer writing the name Kimball on the tab.

He then filed it in the top drawer, with several other folders, behind a red divider labeled – *Delusion of Self-accusation.*

The Set Up...

Sebastian Kimball was prompt for his Thursday appointment, and every Thursday after that for the next month. At his fourth session, Dr. Lockwood shared his diagnosis of delusion of guilt, suggesting an unorthodox treatment program.

"Mr. Kimble I have been pioneering a successful treatment program with other patients who have a delusional diagnosis. I'll be the first to admit it is unconventional, but my success rate has been exceptional. Would you be willing to participate?"

Sebastian looked around the room, his eyes landing on the leather couch. "Are you talking about hypnosis?"

"In a way, yes, but it is not what you think of as traditional hypnosis. It would be done away from this office."

"I'm not sure I'm following you," he said, puzzled.

"I have an attic room in my home that provides just the right conditions - the lighting, the quietness, and even the musty smell all contribute to opening the mind for resolution."

Sebastian hesitated.

"I'm only suggesting it because, after hearing you over the last few weeks, I think you would be a perfect candidate for this treatment. I believe it will help you far more than continuing sessions here in my office."

After thinking about it for a minute, Sebastian responded. "Alright, I'll try it. When do you want to start?"

"Are you working this Saturday? We'll need about two hours to complete a session. Morning or afternoon would be fine. And Sebastian, I'm sure you're going to feel an immediate change."

"No, I'm not working," Sebastian replied, considering what other options he had. "Is eleven o'clock too early?"

"That will be fine Mr. Kimball. I'll write my address on the back of my card for you."

He arrived five minutes before eleven at 632 Tioga Lane, double-checking the address written on the back of the card. The home was an American four-square design, painted light blue with white trim, exhibiting a covered front porch, and a dormer window on the top floor.

Sebastian gingerly rang the doorbell and heard the faint chime inside signal his arrival.

Moments later, the door opened into a vestibule.

"Welcome Mr. Kimball," greeted Dr. Lockwood. "Please come in and go right up these stairs to the top floor. Look around, I'll be with you momentarily."

He then disappeared into the parlor.

Opening the door to the attic space, Sebastian stepped inside. It was very much as you would expect to see. The room was small with open rafters. He could stand, but barely. Boxes appearing to be filled with old clothes, shoes, and books were lined along the outer walls. Stacks of old magazines and newspapers were also piled around the space. A few pieces of wood furniture, consisting of end tables, chairs, a quilt rack, and two chests, were stacked in the corners of the room. Several old pictures hung from the rafters.

A small window, covered by a sun-faded roller shade, let in a dim light that bathed the space in a warm glow. Off to one side, there was a Windsor chair set before a large mirror.

"This isn't what you normally think of when you're going to the doctor, is it?" Doctor Lockwood's voice surprised him.

Sebastian's response came slowly as he looked around the space. "No, not in the least."

"If you're feeling uncomfortable, Mr. Kimble, you don't have to do this," he assured Sebastian.

"No, it's alright. Strangely, I feel very comfortable here. You say others have received treatments here as well?"

You are the fourth person to receive treatment in this room. I'm finalizing my study soon and plan to submit it for review and testing. You are going to be part of history Mr. Kimball, except your name will be omitted for privacy reasons. So in the future, when you hear about this breakthrough technique, you'll know you contributed to it. How does that make you feel?"

"Pretty good I guess... especially if I can get rid of these horrible thoughts I have."

"Well then let's get started. I want you to have a seat in this chair," he said, resting a hand on the Windsor chair.

As Sebastian sat, Dr. Lockwood gave him instructions.

"You'll be looking at your reflection in the mirror. Now I know your attention will be drawn to other things in this room, but just let things take their course. What I want you to do is take time to relax, and then gradually focus your attention on the mirror. It is your image that I want you to concentrate on first, and then mentally describe what you see to yourself. Eventually, everything else in the room will disappear, and you'll just be having that mental conversation with yourself."

"Where will you be while all this is happening?"

"I'll be downstairs should you need me. Now, if you are ready to start, begin by taking slow, deep breaths." The Doctor waited until his patient found a comfortable position and began taking deep breaths, then he quietly stole away.

The first fifteen minutes went exactly as the Doctor described. While taking the deep breaths, Sebastian's curiosity was drawn to the objects in the room. However, he was gradually able to block them out and contemplate his reflection in the mirror. The dim light helped to relax him. The musty smell brought back memories of his childhood. He started to think about things he had not thought of for a long time, which eventually gave way to a reflex conversation with himself.

One hour and forty-five minutes after stepping into the attic, Sebastian found Dr. Lockwood sitting in his parlor reading a book.

"You are finished early," he said, as Sebastian surprised him. "The other patients' first visits lasted almost two and a half hours."

"I don't know what happened. I was thinking about that man in the mirror... uh, I mean *myself*, and I must have fallen asleep. I feel delightfully refreshed. Is that how I'm supposed to feel?"

The Doctor laid his book aside and went over to Sebastian. Laying a hand on his shoulder, he said, "Yes, that can happen the first time. What do you remember?"

"Well I remember taking those deeps breaths, and then I concentrated on my reflection. Soon, everything but that mirror disappeared from the room. It was as if I was floating and just looking at that image of myself sitting in the chair. I think I started to have thoughts about myself but I can't remember what they were."

"Very good. It might take another session before you'll be able to focus and have that inner conversation with yourself, but you did very well."

"When can I come back? I'm anxious to try it again."

"Perhaps next Saturday."

"Next Saturday! No, no, I have to come before then. I felt so good. I really need to come back sooner than that. Won't you please move it to earlier in the week? Any day. I'll change my schedule if I have to."

"Alright, we can do Wednesday," the Doctor agreed, "but not before four o'clock."

"Thank you so much Doctor. You don't know what this means to me."

Meeting the Man in the Mirror...

Wednesday could not come fast enough for Sebastian Kimball. He sat in his car across the street from 632 Tioga Lane for nearly an hour, waiting for his scheduled treatment time. He didn't know if Dr. Lockwood would already be at home or coming from his office, so he watched for any sign of him.

When nothing happened, at exactly at 4 p.m. he went onto the porch, rang the doorbell, and waited to hear movement toward the front door. Still nothing. He pushed the button again and listened to the faint echo of the chime inside the house. Then he heard a lock open and the door handle turned.

"I am sorry, Mr. Kimble, I was in the basement when you first rang. Please, come in."

"Can I go to the attic? I've been feeling anxious over the last few days and I need to sit in that chair."

"Alright, I'll come with you."

"That's not necessary, I know the drill. That is, unless you have something else you want me to know?"

"No, it will be the same as before, but..."

Sebastian did not wait for any further discussion and quickly began his ascent, taking two steps at a time.

A queer smile came across Dr. Lockwood's face.

Within ten minutes, Sebastian fell into his trancelike state. The objects in the room faded and his chair appeared to float. Staring at the mirror in front of him, his image began to appear in the glass, but it was almost as though he had to mentally coax the image to fully reveal itself and he concentrated harder.

"Kimball!"

"*Who said that?*" he asked, startled. The distraction, causing his image in the mirror to weaken.

I must have imagined I heard something, he thought. He then tried to concentrate on bringing back his image.

"Kimball!" The voice spoke again.

"Is someone there? Who called my name?" He probed into the nothingness.

"Kimble, look at me."

Sebastian took up his image in the mirror, and then slowly watched as it morphed into another person, stranger who was seated before him.

Bewildered, but unalarmed, he asked, "Who are you?"

"I am your inner voice, the one you have been listening to all your life. The one you question when you have doubts about making decisions. I'm the reason you sought out Dr. Lockwood to help you understand your thoughts of guilt. I am here to help you."

"Is this real?"

"There can be a fine line between what is real and what one wants to believe is real. If I tell you this is real, would you believe me?"

"Yes, yes I would," he answered without hesitation.

"Then let's go back to when you were fourteen and your mother fell on the stairs. Can you recall that day?"

"Yes, I got off the school bus near my house and, when I went inside, I found my mother at the bottom of the stairs. She was in pain and couldn't move. I called 9-1-1 and they took her to the hospital. Then I called my dad; he picked me up and we went to the hospital together."

"So why then did you feel responsible for her accident?"

"I don't know! I just did."

"What else was going on that day? What happened between you and your mother that morning?"

He gazed into the face of the man in the mirror and felt compelled to tell him everything. "It was nothing. She came into my room to confront me about a pack of cigarettes she had found under my bed. We had a bad argument and she threatened to tell my dad. I was afraid of my dad and what he might do to me."

"So, you are telling me that you didn't hurt your mother. However, maybe you wished something bad would happen to her, so that she wouldn't tell your father?"

"Yes, that's exactly what I thought."

"It's good that you admit that, Kimball. This is how you can heal yourself, by seeing that your thoughts could in no way have harmed your mother. Now tell me about the university student who had the accident."

Sebastian momentarily considered the features of the man in the mirror. Although the image was not crisp, he could see a kind but concerned face compelling him to unburden himself further.

"He told a professor that I cheated on an exam and I got a failing grade for the class. One day I saw him driving off campus and was wishing he'd have an accident. Just then someone rode a bike in front of his car; he swerved and hit a tree head on. I never meant for him to be injured."

The man's voice again filled the space.

"It was just a thought you had; it was just a coincidence. You understand that now, don't you?"

"Yes I do."

"Good! Thinking bad things does not make you a bad person Kimball. Everyone has thoughts like that at one time or another. We'll work on bad thoughts some more when you come back. But right now, I want you to close your eyes, relax, and feel good about yourself."

The voice trailed off while suggesting calm and peaceful thoughts.

Sometime later, Sebastian opened his eyes and, feeling invigorated, departed the attic.

You must have had a good experience... it's seven thirty," said Dr. Lockwood, looking at his watch when Sebastian appeared in the room. "Do you remember anything?"

"Not really. But I feel terribly good about myself right now. It's as if I could do anything and it would not bother me in the least. Is that a good thing?"

"Very good indeed. It means your feelings of guilt are going away, and that is why you came to me, isn't it?"

"Yes. Thank you so much for your help. How soon before I can come back? I have an overpowering need to maintain the sensation these treatments give me, he expressed anxiously, and appearing agitated that he might be kept waiting. "I enjoy being in that room, and the way I feel afterwards. I will do anything to come back. You must make yourself available to me Doctor.

"Alright," the Doctor replied, removing Sebastian's hands, which now gripped his shoulders. "Come back on Friday, around one o'clock. I have another patient that morning at my office."

He showed Sebastian to the door and watched him cross the street to his car.

Acting on Impulse…

On Friday morning, Sebastian watched the rain bead off his car window as he waited for Dr. Lockwood to return home. He had driven around the block several times to help pass the time, and was now nervously drumming his fingers on the steering wheel as the car clock read 1:15 p.m.

A dark sedan turned the corner ahead, slowing as it reached Lockwood's driveway. It pulled into the long drive leading to the garage at the rear of the house.

Sebastian got out of his car and made a dash to the garage, catching the Doctor as he was lowering the garage door.

"You're late!" he accused, the light rain wetting his clothes.

"I'm sorry Mr. Kimball. My other patient took longer than I expected. Please come inside and get in out of the rain."

He led Sebastian up the rear stairs into the house. "Wait here. I'll get you a towel."

When he returned, he could tell that Sebastian was irritated.

"Are you alright? You seem out of sorts." Then he added, "I'm not sure it's a good idea to do a treatment when you are not calm and relaxed."

Sebastian returned a cold stare, responding, "I'm going upstairs. I'll be relaxed when I get there."

He finished drying himself off, threw the towel in the direction of the Doctor, and passed through the kitchen and parlor to reach the stairway. This time it took nearly twenty minutes for him to calm to a point that would allow him to begin to float. His mind eased when the man in the mirror appeared.

"Kimball, you are disturbed today. Why?"

"I needed you... I needed to hear your voice."

"I'm here. Why did you treat Dr. Lockwood that way? He's only trying to help you."

"I don't know. I feel bad about it."

"Don't take your frustrations out on him." The man in the mirror cautioned. "He has his own problems."

"Like what? What could *he* have to be worried about?"

"His ex-wife is giving him grief about selling this house. She's on the deed and wants her share of the money from its sale. If he sells," the man in the mirror continued, "he'll have to stop these treatments and you won't be able to come back here to be with me."

"*I have to come back here!*" Sebastian yelled at the image. "*We can't let her do that!*"

"Do you want to help the Doctor?"

"Yes, anyway I can. *Tell me what to do!*"

"You have to go see her; reason with her. If she doesn't listen, you know what you have to do, Kimball. There is no other way. By helping the Doctor, you are helping yourself. Remember, your mother and that student did not suffer at your hands. And you now know it was okay to have bad thoughts; you know they don't make you a bad person."

Silence followed.

"Are you having bad thoughts about the Doctor's wife?" Solicited the voice.

"Yes, she's a terrible woman. She can't take this house away from us!"

"What else are you thinking? It's alright to think bad thoughts Kimball."

"*I want her to die*! She's has to die to save this house!"

"Kimball, listen closely… here is her address – remember it!"

That night, Kimball knocked on the door of a modest house in the suburbs. A woman answered the door.

"Mrs. Lockwood? You don't know me, but I have to talk to you about your husband, Randolph. It's important. May I come in?"

She stood aside so he could gain entry and closed the door behind him.

"Has something happened to Randy?" she asked, escorting him to a chair in the living room.

"Well to be honest, he has been out of sorts lately. I am worried about him."

She looked inquisitively at her guest. "I'm sorry, I forgot to ask your name?"

"My name is Sebastian Kimball ma'am. I am one of Dr. Lockwood's patients."

He didn't notice her unease at first, but, when he started to talk, she stood and asked him to leave.

"You don't understand ma'am. You can't take that house away from him. It's our home!"

"Look, I don't know who you are or why you are here, but please leave, or I'll have to call the police."

He stood and moved toward her pleading with her to listen to him.

She backed away and started to let out a scream, but Sebastian quickly grabbed the back of her head with one hand while he covered her mouth with the other.

She began to fight him and, in doing so, lost her balance. Slipping from his grasp, she careened over an end table sending a porcelain lamp to the floor and subsequently crashed her head against it as her body followed. Blood flowed from the back of her head and seeped into the carpet. Her frightened eyes stared at the ceiling, but she did not utter a sound. Her body twitched for about thirty seconds, and then all her motion stopped.

"So, as I was saying Mrs. Lockwood," Sebastian continued, "you can't take our house away from us. I hope you understand. Your ex-husband needs to keep that house so that I can continue with my treatments. I really do better when I have them. I'll leave you alone now, and you can think on what I've said. Have a good night, Mrs. Lockwood."

He returned to his car and drove away.

Be Careful What You Ask For...

The violent death of Mrs. Anita Lockwood dominated the next morning's news stories. They reported that a neighbor's dog barked incessantly about 8 p.m., and when the neighbor went outside to see what was causing the commotion, she noticed that Mrs. Lockwood's front door was open. Upon entering her house, the neighbor found the victim in a pool of blood. Police were calling her death suspicious.

Meanwhile, oblivious to the newscasts, Sebastian was readying himself to return to 632 Tioga Lane. He did not recall getting an appointment for a return visit, but assumed he would be able to have another session. After all, it was Saturday, and the good Doctor should be at home. His idea was to go as early as possible, before the Doctor could make any other plans.

At 9:30 a.m. he arrived at the house and pulled into the driveway. Noticing that the garage door was closed, he felt satisfied that he had arrived before Dr. Lockwood could get away.

He knocked on the back door and waited. He knocked again louder and waited.

When no one came to the door, he looked into the garage through the dirty panes of glass and saw that the dark sedan was not inside.

Anxiety overtook him and he ran to the back door. Placing his shoulder against it, he bumped it hard with his body. It opened.

Running through the house, Sebastian climbed the stairs to the attic and sat in the chair. For a full half-hour he tried to visit with the man in the mirror, but nothing happened. Everything in the room was visible to him, and he could not relax sufficiently to make himself and the mirror float. Frustration set in, and then anger.

After a time, he heard footsteps on the stairs ascending to the attic.

"Mr. Kimball, are you there?" called a familiar voice, a voice very similar to the one he heard from the man in the mirror.

"There you are." The Doctor appeared at the top of the stairs. "What did you do to my door?"

"Where were you?" Sebastian's response was terse. "You should have been here to let me in!"

"I was asked to go to the morgue and identify the body of my ex-wife. Don't you know what happened? It has been all over the news."

"I didn't watch the news, and I didn't know you had an ex-wife."

"Sure you did. We talked about her at length."

"I don't remember. And why can't I see the man in the mirror? I have to talk with him."

"Mr. Kimball, you should leave. I'm very distraught about my wife's death, and we can do this another time."

"*No! We have to do it now*! I feel I did something wrong, and only he can help me. He knows I'm not a bad person."

Dr. Lockwood moved to the chair and tried to help Kimball out of it.

Sebastian initially resisted the attempt, and then he suddenly rose up, putting his hands around the Doctor's neck. He squeezed as hard as he could, repeating, "I am not a bad person! I am not a bad person!"

The look in Dr. Lockwood's eyes was one of terror.

The look in Sebastian's eyes was manic as his hands tightly clutched the Doctor's neck, choking the life out of him. Two minutes later, he could no longer manage to hold the Doctor's body. Sebastian let him fall to the floor.

He returned to the Windsor chair and stared into the mirror. His reflection was all that he could see for now, but he patiently waited for the man in the mirror to appear.

Closing Arguments...

"How does your client plead, Counselor?"

"Not guilty by reason of insanity, Your Honor. The defense intends to prove that Mr. Kimball did not have control over his mental faculties at the time of the deaths of Mr. and Mrs. Lockwood. Evidence will show that Mr. Lockwood contributed to his own death."

"Very well. Trial will be set for August fifth. The accused is denied bail and will be remanded to the county until the date of his trial."

Over the next few weeks, details of the defense's evidence were leaked to the press. The killings had caused quite a stir and made national headlines. All the major news outlets brought out their legal and psychological experts to comment on the case, but nothing was called into question more than the methods and techniques used by psychiatry in general.

During pre-trial visits, Kimball's lawyer went into great detail with him about what they had found in the Doctor's basement and attic. Sebastian admitted that he had almost no memory of what happened once he stepped inside the house. He only remembered sitting outside in his car, the garage, and the back of the house.

"I can't defend you against killing those people," acknowledged his lawyer. "The evidence is too strong. However, I seriously doubt that any jury could convict you of murder once we show them what Dr. Lockwood was up to, and that you were not in your own mind when you committed those crimes."

"Tell me again all the things you found out about the Doctor? I'm having a difficult time understanding your line of defense," asked Sebastian.

"Let's start with the police investigation of Mrs. Lockwood's death. They knew she had not died from an accidental fall because of the position of her body relative to where the furniture was located. Then there was the open door and barking dog, implying that there was an intruder. They also lifted fingerprints off the arms of the chair near where her body was found, but didn't know they were your fingerprints until later." The lawyer paused. "Now, in cases similar to these, spouses, exe's, and partners are always considered suspects. So after Dr. Lockwood went to identify his wife's body, the police went to his house to ask him some questions. That's when they saw the broken back door and went inside to make sure that he was alright. They found you sitting in that Windsor chair with his body lying next to you.

"But so far, nothing you've said could vindicate me."

"I'm getting to that. After the police arrested you, the attic was turned into a crime scene where they found all sorts of electronic gear. There was a camera hidden behind one of the old pictures hanging from a rafter, which could view most of the attic, particularly you sitting in that chair and the mirror. Then they discovered that Lockwood had the back of the mirror rigged with some kind of holographic projection system – they're still trying to figure that one out. There was also a miniature microphone and receiver drilled through the corner of the mirror's molding, enabling him to communicate with you. Lastly, there was a tube through which he apparently released a gas that put you in a stupor. That's probably why you can't remember what happened when you were in that room."

"Forgive me, but when you took me back to the attic after my arrest, you mentioned something about the basement."

"The basement was used as his control station. There were TV monitors and control boards through which he could watch, listen, and communicate with anyone in the attic. The gas tube that ran from the attic to the basement was hooked to a small tank from which he could dispense the mind altering substance."

"That's a lot of trouble for someone to go through just to make me crazy, isn't it?"

"But as I told you previously, you weren't the only victim. When the police searched his office, they found the records of three other people who Dr. Lockwood also tried to make them kill his wife. He was probably perfecting his so-called *treatment sessions* with them, but they ended in failures. One was a Mrs. Stouffer, who committed suicide, apparently because she was so overwhelmed by the thought of killing someone else. Then there was Otto Potts and David Gorman. Both men were probably on their way to carry out Dr. Lockwood's wishes, but Potts tried to kill his boss first, and Gorman was arrested for setting fire to a retail store because they wouldn't do a simple refund for him. They have been incarcerated over a year now."

"You mean he used us all just to get rid of his wife?"

"*Exactly*! That way his hands would be clean, because none of you had any memory of your treatments, so you couldn't blame him."

"What about the man in the mirror?"

"It was just a holographic image the Doctor manipulated from the basement. However, there was one common thread between you and his other victims."

"What was that?"

"You all were assessed by him and found to have delusions of guilt or sin. Apparently that's when there is a false feeling of remorse or guilt of delusional intensity. A person may, for example, believe that he or she has committed some horrible crime and should be punished severely. That's why you had those thoughts about your mother, the student, and about the woman who died in the fire at the City Clerk's Office. I'll have an expert testify to how that condition in itself could have been heightened by the good Doctor. Add in the mind-altering gas, and, well, the jury won't have a choice but to consider you insane."

"Does that mean I'll spend the rest of my life in a nut house?"

"Probably for a while Mr. Kimball, but I'll ask that they set you up on a regular testing program. Given time, they'll see that you're not a threat and could consider releasing you."

The day before the trial, Kimball's lawyer went to visit with Sebastian to make final preparations for the court proceedings. When he arrived at the visitation area, the guard, inside the room with Sebastian, let him in. There sat his client on a wooden chair, facing a barred window.

The sky outside was dark, caused by a passing storm, which made the window reflect the light from inside the room. The lawyer noticed Sebastian staring at his own reflection in the window as he approached, but he couldn't quite hear the words his client was muttering to himself.

"I am not a bad person. I am not a bad ..."

END

LAST MAGIC ACT

Tom Shay heard the half-dozen claps as he departed the stage. His ego was intact, that is, until he approached the stage manager.

"Not a good night, Tom," the manager engaged. "What does this one make... your seventy-first appearance?"

"Seventy-second," he responded, peeking into the near-empty gallery of seats just before the curtain closed. His instincts told him where the conversation was headed even before the manager's next words.

"Maybe if you could freshen your act, Tom. You know, add a few new tricks to your routine. The crowd has been falling off for the past twenty shows, I don't know how much longer we can keep you... we're losing money on you."

"You think I've lost it, don't you?"

"No, kid. It's just that for anyone over thirteen, your magic doesn't grab their interest. Even with serving them drinks, your tricks are pretty boring."

"Well, maybe I could introduce a few new illusions."

"Better do it by next week, or we'll have to cut you from the show. You're here as a favor to your uncle. Now *he* knew how to mesmerize a crowd."

Accompanying the young man from the stage, the manager changed the subject, "How is your Uncle Bennie these days, we miss him around here. Too bad he got Alzheimer's."

Fumbling his magic props into a box, Tom replied, "My dad says I better go see him soon. He's been going downhill fast."

The stage manager put a hand on Tom's shoulder. "Too bad he can't teach you some of his old tricks. The crowd is younger than when he entertained on our stage. I think they would respond well to some of the sleight of hand your uncle used back then. Anyway, see what you can do by next week. You'll have one more chance kid. I'll be rooting for you."

The manager gave him a pat on the back then walked over to the next act.

Tom's shoulders rounded as he rested his hands on the sides of the box. His head was bowed showing submission to the manager's request.

I don't think I can learn new tricks in a week, he thought. Maybe I should just quit now.

He finished loading his things into the box and pushed the box on a cart to the side door.

"Hello, Tom, how did it go tonight?" asked the waitress, placing his usual cup of coffee in front of him.

Opening a pouch of sugar, he added it to his cup and slowly stirred it into the liquid before answering. "Not very well, Sherry. I think I'm going to be fired next week if I don't freshen up my act."

"Now Tom, that would be a damn shame. I'd miss you if you didn't come in here every Friday night. What are you going to do?"

"I don't know, Sherry. I don't know."

She patted him on the shoulder then moved off to service another customer.

Gathering the cup in his hands, he moved it to his mouth and let the steam seep into his nostrils. A blank stare fell on the opposite bench seat as he recalled the memory of Uncle Bennie showing him his first magic trick. His uncle had rolled a coin between his fingers and then into the palm of his hand. Then he made a fist and turned it upside down. When he turned his hand over and opened it, the coin was gone. Next, he reached to Tom's ear and tugged on it. When he showed Tom his hand again, the coin reappeared in his uncle's palm. He was only ten at the time, but that started his love for performing magic. Even now, most of the props he used in his act, were given to him by his uncle, along with many hours of training. But, Tom clearly understood the manager's concern about his act going stale. And without his uncle to teach him, he was lost.

"Refill?" Sherry interrupted his memory.

"No thanks. I need to be going. I'll see you next week," he said, laying a five-dollar bill on the table.

Uncle Bennie just sat and stared at his nephew as he always had during Tom's visits to the nursing home. Drool, running down his chin from his slightly open mouth, and an occasional blink yielded the only signs that Bennie was alive. Tom wondered what went through the mind of a person with Alzheimer's or did they even think at all. Nonetheless, he engaged his uncle telling him of the acts he performed on stage and what the stage manager had recently said to him about the next time being his last magic act.

"What do I do, Uncle Bennie? I hate my job, and magic is the only other thing I know. But I'm not as skilled at it as you were." He hesitated, then added, "It's a good thing I live alone, because I could never make a living from it to support a family." Tom chattered on.

After thirty minutes of crying in his beer to his uncle about his lack of proficiency and dismal future, Uncle Bennie startled him. Bennie, in an almost catatonic state, had managed to utter a single word that caught his nephew by surprise.

"What did you say, uncle, I didn't get that."

The old man's chest jerked as he launched the word again, "Wigi!"

"I'm sorry, uncle, did you say w-i-g-i?" Tom leaned toward his uncle turning his best ear for a better chance at hearing him.

There was no further response from Bennie, only his blank stare.

"Wigi, if that's what you said, uncle. I don't know what that means or what it refers to. Did I even hear it right?"

He patted his uncle on the hand. "I'll be back next week. I'll let you know if that was my last magic act."

He then departed from the facility.

#

"How was your uncle today, son?"

"Pretty much the same as usual… he sat there staring and I never knew if he understood anything I said to him. But he surprised me by grunting a word, although I'm not sure I heard it right."

"What did he say, son?"

"I thought he said, wigi, but it wasn't very clear."

Tom's father mouthed the word to himself several times as though he were thinking about something. "Wigi, huh. I wonder if he was trying to tell you about his Ouija board?"

"Ouija board? Why would he say something like that?"

"I don't know, son. But your uncle had an Ouija board since we were kids. I don't even remember where he got it from. He used to go off by himself and play with it for hours."

"Whatever happened to it, dad?"

"It's in the basement somewhere, with all the other things your aunt wanted to get rid of when Bennie went into the home. Maybe he wanted you to have it. Why don't you go and see if you can find it?"

"I think I will. Maybe I can develop some inspiration from it for Friday's show," Tom said, moving toward the basement door.

"I put his boxes along the back wall in the furnace room," his dad yelled, directing him.

Upon reaching the containers that housed his uncle's effects, he rummaged through them hoping he also might come across some of his uncle's old magic tricks.

Tom's disappointment grew with each opened box until he shuffled through to the last one. There, he found his uncle's Ouija board at the very bottom, along with the wooden, heart-shaped planchette that was moved about the board, and pulled them out.

The face of the board game was burnt-orange with black ink lettering and symbols embossed on it. The letters of the alphabet were arranged in an arch pattern in two rows of thirteen letters, with the numbers zero to nine centered below. At the top, were pictures of a sun in one corner with the word 'yes' next to it, and in the opposite corner was a moon with the word, 'no' adjacent. At each of the bottom corners, were the single figures of a magician. They faced each other, as if dueling with their magic wands. The ink on parts of the lettering and numbers were rubbed thin through usage, particularly at the word, 'goodbye' at the bottom of the board.

Tom returned all of his uncle's other belongings to their containers, nestled the Ouija board under his armpit, and returned to his father waiting in the living room.

"I haven't seen that board since I married your mother, son. Your uncle always was secretive with it, and I don't remember him ever sharing it with me. Thinking back, I'd say now that he was sort of creepy about it."

"Do you know how it works?"

"I don't, Tom. I think you just put your hands on the planchette and it's supposed to take you where it wants to go."

"I'll do some research on it. Thanks dad for letting me have it."

"No need to thank me. If your uncle did manage to speak the word, wigi, then it was all his idea, son."

#

Two days later, Tom sat in front of his computer and performed a search on Ouija boards. He clicked on one of the response links titled, *Can You Use an Ouija Board Alone*, and began reading. The article indicated that you could use an Ouija board alone, but because a spirit board has the tendency to attract negative human entities, or worse, a person alone is believed to be in a more vulnerable position for mischief from malicious entities.

Tom adjusted his seat and continued reading: *There is a belief that negative entities are more attracted to people with negative vibrations, such as people who may be bothered or troubled while using the board.* Scrolling farther: *When using a spirit board, turn off all electronic devices so as not to have distractions in the background, which can affect the subconscious mind and the replies you receive to your questions. Put yourself in a calm state and allow the spirits to communicate through your fingertips to the indicator. If you successfully connect with a spirit, ask them for their name and for the name of anyone that sent them. Officially close the board when finished a session by saying the session has ended and no further spirits or contact are allowed. Sweep the planchette over the 'goodbye' symbol on the board, and be sure to cover the board until the next session. There is no guarantee that you will be successful. Sometimes contact occurs quickly, sometimes slowly, and sometimes it doesn't happen at all. Be patient and have fun.*

"Have fun!" Tom sniped under his breath. "Can you call it fun when dialoguing with the spirit world? Do people really take this stuff seriously? I'm sure it's similar to all magic, which uses smoke, mirrors, and sleight of hand to try to deceive audience perceptions."

He placed the board on his kitchen table and the planchette on the board. "I guess I'll give it a whirl," he uttered to himself.

Then he turned off the music he was listening to, pulled the blinds closed, and made himself comfortable in a chair. Placing his hands gently on the wooden planchette, he waited.

After a few minutes, he opened one eye and scanned the room as if looking for someone, or something, to appear. *I must look ridiculous sitting here*, he thought, and closed his eye and concentrated on his fingertips. But nothing happened.

The next day, Tom went to visit his uncle. "I located your Ouija board, Uncle Bennie. Dad had it stored in his basement with your other things. I tried using it a couple of times, but nothing materialized. I was also hoping to find a few tricks in your effects, that perhaps you never shared with me, but I didn't find anything. Instead, I've been playing around with a few ideas I got off the internet, but I'm not sure how well I can do them by Friday's show. I'm afraid it's going to be my last performance, uncle."

After a short visit, Tom said, "I sure wish there was a way to learn some of your skills." He patted his uncle on the back of the hand and said, "I'll be back in a few days to let you know how everything went."

After his nephew departed the room, the old man's chest jerked as he blurted the word, wigi!

###

Friday afternoon, Tom thought he would give the Ouija board another attempt and set it onto the table. When satisfied that he made all the necessary preparations, Tom made himself comfortable and began a session.

At first, the results were the same – nothing. But then, his fingers felt a tug on the planchette and he instinctively asked, "Is someone here?"

The piece moved across the sun symbol and to the word 'yes'.

Anxiously trying to remember the instructions he read on the internet, he asked, "Can you tell me your name?"

The pointer slowly went in order to the letters, D-A-I-M-O-N.

"Daimon, that's a nice name," Tom repeated. "Uh, Daimon," he added, trying to recall the instructions, "did someone send you?"

The pointer again swept across the sun and to the word, 'yes'.

A nervousness feeling came over Tom. "Who?"

The piece moved to the two rows of arched letters and spelled, B-E-N-N-I-E.

"Uncle Bennie sent you! Wow!" He tried to think of his next question. "Why did Uncle Bennie send you?"

The pointer spelled out the word I-N-S-T-R-U-C-T and the word Y-O-U.

"Instruct me, Tom repeated, "Who are you?"

The planchette pulled his hands to the answer, G-R-E-A-T-E-S-T M-A-G-I-C-I-A-N.

Puzzled, Tom asked, "What makes *you* the greatest magician?"

Again, the spirit revealed an answer: T-A-U-G-H-T B-E-N-N-I-E.

After what seemed like only a few minutes, Tom glanced at the clock on the stove. "Six o'clock!" he shouted. "I have to be going! But I have to know when will you teach me?"

T-O-N-I-G-H-T.

He quickly left the board on the table, dressed in his magician's suit, gathered his box of props, and departed his apartment fearing he would be late to his scheduled last appearance.

As soon as Tom locked the front door, the planchette on the board mysteriously moved on its own and swept across the word, 'goodbye'.

At the same time, across town, Uncle Bennie took his last breath.

#

When Tom's last trick ended that evening, the crowd which was fairly large, gave a standing ovation to Tom. He bowed low in acceptance of their appreciation for the performance he gave. At the audience's insistence, he gave a curtain call.

When the curtain finally closed, the stage manager ran over to him and exclaimed, "I can't believe it, Tom. That was the best performance I ever saw you give. I don't know how you learned all that trickery in just a week, *but you were fantastic.* You reminded me so much of your Uncle Bennie and the way he used to present. I can guarantee you'll be back performing that show many times in the coming months."

"Thank you very much for your vote of confidence. You should know, however, that I will be making a name change to the act. You'll need to update your advertising media."

"You mean you're no longer going to refer to it as The Amazing Tom's Magic?"

"That's right, I'm now going to call it, Daimon's Mind-blowing Magic Act."

The manager gazed at Tom with a puzzled look.

END

HALFWAY TO A PROPHESY – THE STONE

The Trip...

"Douglas Peterson, please report to the ticket agent," announced a voice over the airport intercom.

Douglas had been waiting at gate 33B in the Houston airport for well over an hour hoping to get on a TACA airlines flight to Lima Peru as a standby passenger. He was hopeful that broadcast signaled good news.

He was taking advantage of a college break, having booked a five-day, four-night package to visit Suntur, an archaeological site built by the Chanka people of Peru. As an archaeology student at George Washington University, he was fascinated by the idea of exploring the ruins of ancient civilizations, but even more so with their cultures. The Chanka people had become one of his foremost study subjects and they were to form the basis of his graduating thesis.

Douglas was a believer that there was a power in the universe which could be harnessed and used for evil or good. He also believed that whoever was in control of the power, determined the outcome. From his research as a graduate student, it was evident that Chanka power rested with the priests of the ancient ones - the source of their power being drawn from the heavens above. He was determined to learn as much as he could about this particular site and the significance it played in Peruvian culture.

Doug went over to the gate desk and produced his identification.

"Mr. Peterson, we have a seat for you on the next flight to Lima," said the agent, passing him the document. "Here is your boarding pass. Seat 16B. You may board now. Have a good flight sir."

She moved on to the next person whose name they called over the intercom.

Leaving the wait area, he made his way along the gangway and boarded the jet. A few hours later he arrived at Jorge Chavez International Airport.

After gathering his luggage, he worked his way through the throng of travelers, and their waiting family members, to locate a cab. His destination was the El Grande hotel in downtown Lima. He planned on spending the night there and then boarding a bus the next morning for the city of Andahuaylas. From there, it was a short, tour-bus ride to the Suntur ruins.

Suntur had been home to the Chanka people from about 1000 to 1450 AD, before they were conquered by the Incas.

Following a wild cab ride from the airport to the El Grande hotel, Doug was ready to relax and experience the sights and sounds of Lima night life. He hoped his rudimentary knowledge of the Spanish language would be sufficient to guide him to a nice restaurant and local music. His luck held through the evening, as his broken Spanish was met with equally broken English by those that provided him the services he wanted to experience.

When morning arrived, with the help of hotel staff, he was directed to the local bus station where he was able to secure round-trip passage from Lima to the city of Andahuaylas. During the six-hour bus ride to his destination, Doug made good use of his time by reviewing his trip itinerary and making his own detailed notes, which would later become part of his final thesis.

Arriving mid-afternoon, Doug's expectations of Andahuaylas were soon revealed. As depicted on the maps, it was a very long town that spread out along the Rio Chumbao River. It was a city of almost 30,000 inhabitants surrounded by mountains, which provided a spectacular scene.

He checked into a small hotel, near the center of town, and then took a walking tour of the area being sure to stop at a few shops for the mandatory souvenirs. His day was topped off by having dinner in an open-air café, indulging in local wines, and appreciating the near full-moon that rose between two mountain peaks.

Sunday came too early for Doug as he nursed a headache from either the altitude, the wine, or both. He had timed his trip so that he could visit the Sunday market, and readied himself as best as he could before he ventured out of the hotel.

Transportation quickly arrived.

The taxi driver asked, "Mercado?"

Doug nodded an affirmative and they took off.

The taxi was well-used, reeking of smoke and cheap alcohol. Between the smell and the driving skills of the driver, he almost threw up. The driver barely spoke more than a handful of words to Doug as he sped to a drop-off point near the market and then raced back for another load of tourists.

Sunday market was billed as one of the biggest and most colorful markets in Peru. It was located along the river at the east end of town. With nearly all of the participants, save for handfuls of tourists, being native Quechua indigenous people, it was a photographer's dream. Their colorful attire and whimsical interaction provided plenty of opportunity to capture the essence of the market. While Doug's skills as a photographer were considered weak at best, he felt qualified to capture inspiring scenes that he would later use as a basis for his thesis. He spent the better part of the day photo journaling his visit.

Nearing 5 p.m., Doug made his way back to the taxi drop-off point. Along the way, he saw a young man emphatically hailing him over to his market booth. Although it had been a long day, he couldn't keep himself from wanting to know what the man was so excited to sell. The salesman was very animated in the way he moved, and his sales pitch was in both Spanish and broken English as he tried to sell Doug a bottle of snake oil potion for treating all manner of ailments.

Without thinking, Doug asked him if he had something for headaches. The man quickly produced a small, cobalt-blue bottle of elixir, which he promised would take care of any size headache, all for the sum of only thirty Sol, or about ten U.S. dollars.

Doug made the deal and tucked the elixir into his backpack, quickly returning to the taxi area for the return trip to the hotel. His taxi experience was as equally a finger-gripping ride as when he arrived that morning.

His evening plan was to retire early in order to be fresh for the morning excursion to the ruins. He ate a light dinner, refraining from drinking wine, so he did not have to test the properties of the elixir he had purchased at the market.

###

At 9 a.m. the next morning, he and a small group of tourists were met in the lobby of the hotel by a tour bus guide. The guide passed out maps of Suntur ruins and nearby Lake Pacucha while he gave a brief overview of what the group was going to see. He then led them out to their transportation.

The bus was blue and white. A vintage, 1960's machine, which didn't appear to be able to drive down the street, let alone, to the ruins. But the tour guide gave an excited invitation for everyone to board so that they could head off to the Chanka stronghold.

Once the bus began to roll, the guide began relaying elements of Chanka history. Some of what he said ringed true to Doug, based on his research, but other parts seemed to have added embellishment. Doug chose not to disclose any of his misgivings about the guide's qualifications on the subject to his fellow tour group members. Instead, he spent the time watching the passing countryside through the open window, and tried to imagine ancient peoples traveling the road to Suntur.

Suntur Ruins...

Arriving at the disembark location, about a quarter-mile from the entrance to the ruins, the guide ushered them over to a nearby concession stand and suggested they buy snacks and water to take along to the ruins. It almost appeared as though the local entrepreneur was a family member of their guide, and they were in cahoots to sell to the tour groups that came through the area. Doug settled for a bottle of water, even though his guide was making suggestions to everyone on what to buy.

From where Doug stood, Suntur was a stunning mountaintop setting; grassy fields hugged the steep slopes below, and, beyond, mountains soared above river valleys on either side. Rings of fallen stones rising to the top suggested that in its history, fortified walls once defended the site. Downhill from the Suntur ruins was a view of Lake Pacucha. Their guide had indicated that the bus would take them to the lake after they had spent sufficient time at the ruins. Quaint adobe settlements and fields dotted the fringes of the ruins' hillside.

The tour guide soon walked the group to the entrance of the ruins and introduced them to another guide. This guide was an old man, but his age was hard to guess as most people here had deep, tanned, wrinkle-etched faces. He was wearing a straw cowboy-style hat, a black long-sleeve shirt covered by a grey and white designed serape, grey pants, and well-worn brown cowboy boots.

He seemed to take a special interest in the presence of Douglas as he said something in Spanish to the bus driver, and then led the group up stone stairs to the top of the ruins. Along the way he pointed out the stone walls that ringed the hill and explained their use.

When they arrived near the top of the hill, they saw two stone buildings with thatched roofs. The old man explained that these were reconstructions to represent the holy place. He followed with an oratory, in broken English, telling of the ancient people of Chanka. Then he invited the group to go inside the larger of the two buildings and 'feel' the presence of the spirits.

When members of the party started to go inside, the old man pulled on the arm of Douglas, beckoning Doug to follow him. He then led him a short distance to a pile of rocks. He reached into his pants pocket and pulled out a thin, smooth stone about two inches long and handed it to Douglas.

Following a puzzled look to the guide, Douglas's attention turned to the stone as he examined it with his hand and fingers. Upon turning it over, he saw a faint image of a condor etched into the rock. He surmised that at one time the etching was deeper, but probably had been worn by frequent rubbing over its surface.

"What's this?" He asked, examining the stone.

"I am to give it to you," the guide answered.

Douglas could see an intensity on the face of his guide and knew that he had more to say.

"So what is this about?" He asked with an equal intensity.

Removing the straw hat from his head and wiping his brow with his shirt sleeve, the man looked over Doug's shoulder at the distant mountains before speaking.

"Do you hear that, señor?"

Doug listened but his gaze stayed on the man in front of him.

"I don't hear a thing other than the wind blowing past my ear. What am I supposed to hear?"

"Close your eyes and really listen, señor. Hold the stone between the palms of your hands," he simulated, "and listen."

Reluctant to shut his eyes, Doug nevertheless felt compelled to follow the instructions and did as he was told. After a few seconds, it appeared to him that the stone grew warmer, and his attention turned solely to the action happening between his hands. Soon, no longer aware of outside distractions, he heard a faint sound and listened intently. The sound grew a louder until he could distinguish it as the melodious sound of a flute. He mentally drew from his antiquity studies, believing the music was being played on an ancient instrument used by the Chankas during their ceremonies. For a moment, Doug's senses were entranced and he felt as though his earthly bonds were broken and he could... A noticeable grin appeared on his face. As quickly as the sound appeared, it softened until he could no longer hear it.

He reluctantly opened his eyes and stared into the wrinkled face of his guide.

"What did I just experience?"

"You heard the ancient bone flute that plays the music to heal the sick. The stone is comparable to your modern-day cell phone - it calls and plays the music. But the music only comes to those that are righteous, and only the righteous can activate the stone's properties."

"I felt it get warm in my hands just before I heard the music. Is that how it works?"

"Yes."

"So why did you pull me aside to show me this?"

"The stone calls for its next owner. That is why you are here; to receive the gift that rightfully belongs to you. You have been a student of the ancient ones and they wish to pay homage to you and for the work you are yet to do."

"So what *am I* to do with it?"

"There will come a time when you will become gravely ill. Because you are a righteous person, the stone will save your life. All you have to do is what you just did – hold the stone between the palms of your hands and listen. When the music stops, you will be cured. But, the stone only works one time. It will disappear from you and return here to me so that I can give it to the next owner. This is the way it has been for over five hundred years."

"Are you a priest? Shaman?"

"I am the descendant of a Chanka priest and keeper of the stone. I work here to fulfill my destiny so that when I pass, I will live in the sun's warmth."

"This is unbelievable," Douglas said, placing the stone in his pocket. Then fumbling with his camera, he asked, "May I take your photograph? It would be a wonderful addition to my collection."

"Please señor. I would prefer you not do that", he said, putting his hands toward his face. "Take the stone and enjoy exploring the rest of the ruins with your companions. I will escort you all back to the bus in about two hours."

He shooed Douglas in the direction of the larger building where the others had gathered.

Doug turned to rejoin his tour group, but after a few steps he thought to ask another question of the guide and turned back around. The guide was nowhere to be seen; it was as though he vanished into thin air.

The young archaeology student spent the next hour photographing everything he could and entering rudimentary calculations of the site into a journal. When the time came to leave, the guide reappeared and gathered the tour group, then he herded them down the hill toward their waiting bus.

After taking his seat, Douglas's eyes caught the figure of his guide through the open window. The old man was helping another passenger board the bus, so he pulled out his camera and took a quick snapshot of them. He didn't want to be denied having the guide's image to go along with the story he would tell everyone about the stone. Unconsciously, his hand brushed across his pant leg to verify that the stone object was still nestled in his pocket.

As the bus pulled away from the site, Doug joined in with everyone onboard waving farewell to their ruins' host and bidding him farewell.

The old man politely returned their wave and gave a final look to Douglas just as another tour bus arrived.

The group was driven to Lake Pacucha where they disembarked at a quaint lakeside eatery called La Cocina por El Lago to lunch on authentic Peruvian food. The fare consisted of measured portions of a salad of Peruvian lima butter beans and ceviche, which was made from chunks of raw white fish marinated in lemon juice, onions and chilies. Another dish was shredded chicken cooked with a sauce of milk, onions, chilies, garlic, walnuts and cheese served over rice. For dessert, the group ate picarones, which are a type of pumpkin fritters normally served with syrup on top. Doug tried everything, helping himself to two servings of the ceviche, which barely allowed him room for the dessert.

With the day ending, Doug was the last person of his group to be dropped off at his hotel. It would be a short evening for him, as he packed his belongings for the six-hour ride back to Lima.

Returning Home…

The next day, Doug made good use of his time on the return trip to Lima by cataloging the photos he had taken and subsequently downloaded to his lap top computer. He made notes alongside each photograph, corresponding them to the format of his thesis. When he came to the photo he thought he had taken of the Suntur guide, only the passenger who the guide had helped board was visible in the picture. Doug thought that odd but decided that, in his haste to grab a photo of the old man, he must have snapped the lens before the old man was fully into the scene. It was a loss he greatly regretted.

After finishing his cataloging, Doug removed the stone from his pocket and set his gaze on it. He found it difficult to comprehend the meaning behind it all; why he was the recipient and the guide foretelling that he would become fatally ill, but that the stone would cure him. But Douglas never gave that thought any true consideration. At best, he surmised that the guide had used that story a number of times to at least one person of a tour group to give them something to talk about. It made for good drama, as he passed them a stone such as the one he now held in his hand. Still, something about that man was eerie.

Rolling the stone through his fingers, under his breath he said, "Nothing special about this. I imagine they make them by the hundreds. This talisman doesn't fit any known object ever discovered from the Chanka culture, so I'm sure it was all made up for my benefit."

He then casually transferred the piece to a pocket inside his backpack and never gave it another thought until he emptied his belongings when he returned home.

#

Six months after the Peruvian trip and completing all his doctoral requirements, Douglas turned in his thesis. The professor rewarded his efforts by giving him the highest grade of all the doctoral candidates. So impressed was his professor on the thesis, he set up a meeting between Douglas and a project director from the Belizean Regional Archaeology Center who was scheduled to visit the Washington D.C. area.

After meeting with Mr. Peterson, the director offered Douglas an Associate Professorship position on the project, which he gladly accepted. Doug spent the next seven years in Belize doing the thing he loved most in the world - exposing college students to the ancient Mayan wonders.

When he developed a chronic upper respiratory infection caused by sustained exposure to high altitudes, he was forced to leave the project. Reluctantly, he accepted the position of administrator of a new museum in Canton, Ohio.

#

Over the next two years, Doug turned into a brooding man. His first love, archaeology, had been taken away from him by poor health. His previous happy-go-lucky attitude was replaced by an ill-tempered arrogance. Now, with an open distaste for administrating the museum's business, he regularly was a topic of conversation among the museum's board members. Eventually they had no choice but to let him go.

Now down on his luck, and without many places to turn to for employment, Douglas found himself in the driver's seat of a forklift. Most of the workers at the regional warehouse where he worked stayed away from him – he was bad Karma.

As his health continued to deteriorate, Doug was forced to make frequent visits to his doctor for treatment of his nagging respiratory condition. The doctor eventually sent him to a specialist. Through the use of low-dose spiral CT scans and examining samples of Doug's sputum under a microscope, the specialist concluded that Doug had developed lung cancer. Speculation centered on Doug's warehouse job and that he may be exposed continually to materials which further aggravate his already delicate condition. The plan was to treat the cancer aggressively. The doctor further suggested Douglas make a change in employment.

The news devastated Doug and he went home that night fearing the worst, that he was going to die. Then he suddenly remembered the stone that he had been given, and the old guide's words about becoming ill.

He frantically searched his belongings looking for the stone, eventually finding the talisman in the bottom of a wooden box he used to store his Peruvian artifacts. Picking it up and holding it between the palms of his hands, he closed his eyes and listened.

Nothing happened.

"I knew that was a lot of bullshit," he said in a disgusted voice.

He tried again. Still nothing happened.

At the same time, he glanced into the box and noticed the bottle of elixir he had purchased from the man at the Andahuaylas market. It had never been opened. Although the contents were old, he thought maybe he could find relief from the pain he felt in his chest. After struggling to remove the cap, he took a drink. At first, it tasted sweet, then his mouth and throat began to burn from the aftertaste of a strong pepper. He ran for the kitchen and downed two glasses of water to try and quell the fire.

"Damn, that stuff tastes bad. I hope it doesn't make me worse than I already am," he said, flushing the remaining liquid into the drain.

The following week, he returned to his doctor's office for his monthly health check on the condition of his cancer. His doctor returned from the lab excited about the outcome of Douglas's x-ray and sputum test.

"I don't want to get your hopes up, but something remarkable has happened... your condition has improved. However, for now, I would put it in the category of false-negative readings. The improvement in your cells may be nothing more than an anomaly. I'll have a better idea next month, if the tests show you have continued to improve."

Immediately, Doug's mind flashed back to that strange elixir he had drank, and wondered if that could have had some healing properties in it after all. Although having dumped the contents, he had kept the bottle because of its pretty cobalt-blue color. He needed to read the information on the label as soon as possible.

The second he arrived home, Douglas fished around in his box until he found the bottle. He picked it up and looked at the label. It was written in Spanish. He could decipher only a few words but stopped when he saw the words, *Corteza Peruana*.

"Peruvian Bark," he muttered. "That has long been used as a home remedy to treat a variety of illnesses. From the spicy taste, I'm guessing that whoever created the concoction added hot pepper sauce, which also has healing properties."

He recalled an internet article he once read, which had stated that the capsaicin and lycopene in peppers may help to inhibit cancer cell growth.

I wonder, he thought. *Could it be?*

#

On his next monthly visit, the doctor returned with the test results to an anxiously awaiting Douglas.

"I wish I had better news for you Doug, but there hasn't been a significant change in the cancer cells, from last month."

"That's a good thing isn't it? I mean the results aren't any worse are they?"

"No, but that could change by your next visit. All we can do is keep monitoring you."

As Douglas departed the office, he knew what he had to do.

Prophesy Fulfilled...

Once again, Douglas found himself leaving the lobby of El Grande hotel in downtown Lima and boarding the bus that would take him to the city of Andahuaylas. Barely outside the limits of Lima, the memory of his last trip to the city flooded his consciousness. He could almost recall every turn the bus would make as it traveled along the road.

Six hours later, he checked into the same small hotel he had previously stayed at in Andahuaylas. Except for a fresh coat of paint, it was exactly as he had remembered. There was time for dinner and a short stroll through the area before he retired for the night.

#

The next day, Sunday market awaited him. He gathered his backpack and placed the cobalt-blue bottle he had brought with him inside. He didn't think he would be able to describe it sufficiently to the market vendors, so he had instinctively brought it along to show them and was hopeful he could pick up several more bottles to take home.

Even at the early hour, the market was bustling with activity. Unlike, his previous visit ten years ago, there were considerably more tourists mixed in among the native Quechua inhabitants. He thought he detected a variety of European accents, as well as, visitors from Asia, as he made his way to the tables that displayed anything in a bottle.

For over an hour he moved throughout the market holding up the bottle and asking the vendors, "Donde puedo encontrar esto?" *Where can I find this?*

Each time, the response was a shrug of the shoulders and a look of, I don't know.

Overcome with emotion that he had wasted his time, he lost his temper and shook a table sending merchandise flying. When he was suddenly surrounded by a group of local vendors, he offered money to pay for damages.

Arriving back at his hotel, he was feeling sick. It was a sickness brought on by failure, rather than a physical ailment. Then he noticed the familiar blue and white vintage bus that took visitors to the Suntur ruins. He quickly secured a ticket and got onboard. The driver was a different person than he remembered from the previous tour, but as they moved over the dirt road to the ruins, the scenes out the window were familiar and gave him a calming effect. For a moment, it was as though he was reliving his first ride.

Reaching the disembark location, he ignored the driver's insistence that the tourists pick up snacks and water at the nearby concession stand. Instead, Doug headed for the entrance to the ruin. He stopped in his tracks when he spotted a familiar figure. At the entrance stood an old man, dressed in a black, long-sleeve shirt covered over by a grey and white designed serape, grey pants, well-worn brown cowboy boots, and wearing a straw cowboy-style hat. Doug walked to him.

"Buenas Dias, Señor. I've been expecting you," the old man said in half-broken English.

Douglas pulled the smooth, round stone from his pocket.

"You lied to me!" He screamed. "There is no magic cure in this stone! You said I was going to become gravely ill and I have. I have lung cancer! You said the stone would save my life… that all I had to do was hold the stone between my palms and listen for the music and then I would be cured. Well that hasn't happened. I believe you put a curse on me instead and I demand you remove it."

Calmly, the old man removed his hat, turned toward the top of the mountains, and then reengaged with Douglas.

"The spirits have spoken, Señor. You are no longer righteous. The stone cannot give healing to a black soul."

The old man turned away and walked up the hill toward the larger of the two buildings.

Frozen in place, Douglas mulled over the guide's words: *black soul*. Deciding he was not going to be denied an explanation, Doug followed after him.

He found the guide standing silently in the middle of the building with his arms outstretched. He had dropped his straw hat onto the dirt floor and stood with eyes closed. Unexpectedly, a low chant started to fill the room.

"*What do you mean I have a black soul?*" Doug yelled.

The chanting grew louder.

Douglas held his hands over his ears to block out the pain that began to sear into his head.

"*Stop that!*" He shrieked, grabbing the old man and spinning him around. "*Tell me what you meant!*"

The old man's eyes remained closed and he continued to chant, causing the throbbing to intensify in Doug's head.

When Doug couldn't take it any longer, he put his hands around the neck of the old man and started to squeeze with all the strength he could muster and screamed, "*Stop it! Stop it!*"

The agony subsided as he felt the old guide go limp; his unsupported weight crashing to the dirt.

Doug panicked and went outside to throw up.

Soon, the group of bewildered tourists arrived at the top. A young man ran over to Doug and offered his assistance.

"I'm a nurse; are you alright?"

"I think I killed him," Douglas said, to his own amazement.

"Who?"

"The old man inside." He pointed.

The young man motioned for another tourist to check inside the temple while he attended to Douglas.

When the woman returned, she said, "There's no one in there."

Douglas pushed past them and went to look for himself.

Half a dozen tourists followed.

One of them made a circling motion with his fore-finger pointed at his own head to the others in the group, seeing that the room was empty.

"I have to find him!"

Doug left the building and went alone to the far side of the smaller structure. Out of view of the others, he pulled the stone from his pocket and held it between his hands. Sobbing he tried to concentrate and listen.

A few minutes later, and standing in the same area where Douglas was last seen moving to, the puzzled nurse said to one of the tour members, "Where did that fellow go? We saw him walk behind this building."

All the members of the visiting group searched every possible location in and around the buildings and nearby stone walls, but saw no sign of Douglas.

The bus driver also assisted with the search, but as the sun was beginning to set, he ushered the group back to the bus, advising they would notify the authorities in Andahuaylas.

The next day, the police, accompanied by the bus driver and nurse, arrived at Suntur ruins. Standing at the entrance was the wrinkled face of the old guide.

"We thought something happened to you," the nurse said. "Yesterday, that strange man on the bus with us said he did something bad to you, but he's disappeared. Have you seen him?"

The old man shook his head indicating no.

The police and bus driver started to climb to the top of the hill.

When the nurse began to follow, the old man grabbed his arm and stopped him. Then, the guide reached into his pocket and pulled out a thin, smooth stone about two inches long and handed it to him.

END

JOY

Doug and Miriam were planning to travel from their home in Austin, Texas to visit Miriam's Aunt Betty, who lived in Oklahoma City. They hadn't seen her in years, and she was getting on in age. Miriam felt they owed her a visit, because she was the only remaining relative of her aunt.

The trip normally took the average driver about six and a half hours. But Doug, being a careful driver, planned on an eight-hour trip, which included stopping for gas and a meal break.

Interstate-35 was not known for its scenery. With the exception of going through the larger cities of Waco and Fort Worth, the route offered nothing visual to help pass the time. The scenery would become particularly boring once they reached Oklahoma. From there, it was cattle country almost all the way to Oklahoma City. Road kill and the birds of prey they drew would likely provide the only entertainment on their journey.

The morning of departure, they called Aunt Betty and told her to expect them around dinner time. Miriam had politely asked her aunt not to make a fuss with dinner, knowing they would arrive too late for her aunt to cook. Miriam advised her they would eat along the way, but that they would enjoy sharing dessert with her when they arrived. Her aunt was known for always having rhubarb pie available whenever a friendly face came to visit.

Doug and Miriam finished packing their car at 9:45 A.M. Before departing, Doug took one last look around their home to make sure all the windows and doors were locked, Miriam's candles were extinguished, and there was no running water anywhere. 'Can't be too safe' was Doug's motto.

When satisfied, Doug joined his wife waiting in their sedan.

As they backed out of the driveway, Doug pressed the button to close the garage door. Miriam busied herself organizing the reading material that would be needed for those long, lonely stretches of I-35.

After one final look at their home, they finally were on their way.

Their first stop was on the north side of Fort Worth to refuel. At Miriam's insistence, Doug never let the gas gauge read below a quarter tank. The fuel stops also provided them time to stretch, take a restroom break, and grab a cold drink. Soon, they were off again.

I-35's lack of character didn't disappoint them; it was to be a very boring drive through each of Oklahoma's southern counties. Almost six hours into their trek, Doug, who was fighting the glare of the sun and corresponding road fatigue, viewed a welcome sight. Ahead, he saw a cloud bank that promised him relief from the punishing sunlight. Eager to reach the shadow line cast across the highway by the clouds, he increased his speed.

When their car entered the shade provided by the cloud, he noticeably felt the temperature drop against the driver's window. The change in conditions agreed with him and gave him renewed vigor. Doug typically preferred driving on overcast days, as long as they were not accompanied by heavy downpours.

After only a few miles of driving under the clouds, rain began to fall. The rain was gentle but steady, and typical for that time of year.

About the same time as the shower began, Doug thought it was time to locate a place to eat. A roadside advertisement soon caught his attention: *The Joy of Eating Cafe - Where We Serve a Heap of Friendliness with your Meal. Take the Joy exit and go east two miles.*

"Honey, we just passed a sign with a suggestion on where we can stop to eat. There's a town ahead named Joy, and they have a cafe there. What do you think?"

Miriam looked up from her magazine long enough to see a road marker indicating that the exit for Joy was in eight miles.

"Sounds okay to me," she responded "it's a good time for us to be stopping anyway. How's the gas?"

"A little less than half a tank. We can fill it when we get there."

Miriam's attention quickly returned to the glossy pages of her magazine, while Doug watched for the upcoming exit.

The road to Joy was a two-lane, blacktop, side road that had seen better days. It was in serious need of repair causing Doug to have second thoughts about continuing. Fortunately, the rain had stopped, which was the only thing in his favor, and he continued.

As he maneuvered around a bend in the road, a small cafe appeared about a block ahead on his left. He called Miriam's attention to the approaching building and she laid aside her reading material.

He pulled into the parking area outside a restaurant that was in the middle of nowhere, and observed the structure. It was a long, white clapboard, single-story building with five windows facing the road. One window was located to the left of the entranceway and four to the right. A large sign over the doorway, and detailed in blue lettering, was inscribed with the business name and motto exactly as he saw on the media sign along I-35.

Miriam peered through the car window. "Doug, are you sure it's open? There are no other cars here."

He shrugged. "It's probably a mom and pop place and they park in back. Look, the sign in the window is lit up indicating they're open. I'll try the door; you wait here."

He got out of the vehicle and pulled on the restaurant's door handle. It promptly swung open, so he beckoned for his wife. As soon as she joined him, they went inside.

They were immediately met by a bubbly woman who greeted them as if they were family.

"We didn't think you were open from the look outside," said Doug, scanning the interior.

The woman smiled. "It's a slow time for us, but don't you worry, we'll be hopping by six o'clock. Where may I sit you folks?" she invited.

Doug looked to his right. "Is that seat by the window okay, honey?"

His wife nodded in agreement and followed his lead.

As she slid into the booth, she surveyed the restaurant's decor. "Cute place!" She emphasized to the woman.

"Yes, we like it - that is, my husband and I. He's the cook here. But he let me have full choice over what I wanted to do with this side of the kitchen. The bar over there," she turned and pointed, "came from an old west saloon that was in a mining town in Colorado. Those bold, brass sconces you see along the walls are from a bordello that used to be in Oklahoma City. And the wood flooring was salvaged from the deck of an early nineteen hundred paddlewheel boat. Everything else was bought or made new a few years ago when we opened, but we tried to keep the look of an old-time place."

"It's kind of odd, but in a nice way," Doug said. "I feel very much at home here. Don't you, Miriam?"

"Yes, it's very quaint and, once you get inside, very comfortable."

The woman changed the subject while handing them menus. "Our specials today are the finest meat loaf you would ever want to put in your mouth and our tender roast beef. We have lots of other wonderful things on the menu too. May I take your drink order while you decide?"

Doug considered the ornate bar across the room lined with colorful bottles of alcohol and beer dispensers. "The bar looks tempting, but I have quite a way to drive yet, so I better have iced tea instead."

Miriam duplicated his drink order, which sent the woman to fill their request.

"This place is very unique," Doug insisted, as he took the woman's history of the place into account. "I wished we lived closer; I'd come here all the time. And our hostess is so nice and interesting. I'll bet you could talk to her all day long."

Miriam was in complete agreement with her husband, and was glad they had traveled the few miles off I-35 to have their dinner.

The woman quickly returned, drinks in hand. "Here's your tea... where are you folks from?"

Miriam took her glass from the woman. "We're from Austin and we're going to Oklahoma City to see my aunt. We're long overdue to visit with her...."

Oh, I'm so sorry," she said, placing the tea in front of her. "Where are my manners? I'm Miriam Robertson and this is my husband, Douglas."

She reached her hand out in introduction.

"Nice to meet you folks!" The woman said, reciprocating the shake. "I'm Doris Tripp, and the cook's name is Sebastian," she said, while thumbing over her shoulder to the back of the cafe. "He'll come out and say hello after you've tried his cooking. Be honest with him though, he doesn't cotton to being placated about his food."

She took out her order pad, "Have you decided what you would like to try?"

"I'll do the meatloaf with mashed potatoes and gravy, and whatever vegetable you have," Doug said, closing his menu.

"And you, Miriam?" the waitress solicited.

"I'll try the roast beef with a baked potato, and a side salad with oil and vinegar dressing."

"Excellent choices - you won't be disappointed, folks. I assure you." The woman gathered their menus and took off in direction of the kitchen.

"This is really a great place," said Miriam, reaching for her husband's hand, "but I'd like to know why there is no one else here? It's almost four-thirty in the afternoon."

"Well, she did say things pick up around six o'clock. Too bad we won't be here then. I figure we have a little more than an hour yet to get to Oklahoma City, and we wouldn't want to keep your aunt waiting. So, we'll eat quickly and then be on our way."

While waiting for their food, the couple sat in their booth discussing stories the bar, wall sconces, and floor could tell if they were people.

"Whose feet walked the deck of that boat?" Asked Miriam, looking at the floor.

"How about what the wall sconces would have to say about the *good* men of Oklahoma City," he added, chuckling.

Doris soon returned and served them their dishes. "Here you go, folks. Sorry it took so long. I know you need to be going soon, but enjoy!"

Doris disappeared into the back room again, leaving them to decide if the meal was worthy of their stopping at The Joy of Eating Cafe.

After about fifteen minutes, Doris reappeared. This time with her husband, Sebastian.

He shook their hands as Doris introduced them. "Well, what did you think of our house specialties?" He invited.

Doug slipped his napkin across his mouth before speaking. "Your wife said we needed to be honest with you and I have to tell you that was absolutely the best meatloaf I've ever eaten. There's some ingredient in there that makes it taste different than I've ever had before. I can't quite put my finger on it," he said, looking to Sebastian for the answer.

"And you, ma'am?" the cook asked. "How was your roast beef?"

"Sebastian, it is s-o-o tender, and I didn't notice any gristle in it. I cut it with only my fork and it practically melted in my mouth. I wouldn't have any idea how you were able to get it that tender," she begged.

"Every cook has secret recipes," he said to them. "And you know it just wouldn't be a secret if I told everyone what they were. But I'm glad you enjoyed what I made for you. Thank you for stopping by and visiting with us. I hope you tell your friends we're here; we love meeting new people. Take care now. Maybe we'll see you on your way back home."

He returned to the kitchen.

After Doris completed the billing transaction for them, they said their goodbyes at the front door.

Before departing, however, Doug asked where the nearest gas station was located.

Doris instructed that it was five miles farther north on I-35.

Reluctant to leave, Doug and Miriam vowed to return, as the three of them waved a final goodbye to one another.

With The Joy of Eating Cafe in his rearview mirror, Doug rounded the bend in the road and soon found I-35. They headed north.

It had been exactly five miles when they saw an exit with a gas station.

After topping off his tank, Doug went inside to pay his charge. He couldn't help dialoguing with the clerk about what a nice restaurant there was down the road. "We just had the best meal at The Joy of Eating Cafe south of here. I'm sure you've eaten there yourself."

The clerk gave a puzzled look at the man standing in front of him, then answered, "Yeah, I haven't eaten there for almost two years, but the food was always good. Too bad about what happened to it."

Doug was now the one with a puzzled look as he asked, "What do you mean?"

"It burnt completely to the ground a few days after my last meal there. The real tragedy was the loss of its owners, Doris and Sebastian. Apparently they tried fighting the fire, but never came out. Their bodies were found in the kitchen.

They really loved that place, and everybody within fifty miles loved them."

"You're wrong!" Blurted out Doug. "We just came from there! Doris and Sebastian are just fine!"

"Uh, sorry, sir, but that's not possible. It's not...."

Before the clerk could utter another word, Doug dashed out to the car, and without comment to Miriam, took the turn going south on I-35.

Miriam could see that he was extremely upset. "What are you doing, Doug? What happened back there?"

"T-h-a-t m-a-n back there," he stuttered. "He said The Joy of Eating Cafe caught fire two years ago and that the owners died in the fire. I don't believe it! We're going right back there!"

He flew along the highway until he reached the Joy exit. He passed over the broken parts of the road leading to the restaurant driving as a madman, only slowing to maneuver around the bend in the road that preceded the cafe. After rounding the bend, his vehicle came to an abrupt stop.

There, in front of Miriam and Doug, lay the ruins of the cafe. Just as the clerk had said, it appeared to have been fully engulfed in a fire. Weather had taken an added toll on the building remnants. Even now, drops from the recent rain dripped from the few charred, wooden posts that still stood erect.

Doug looked at Miriam and she returned his equally blank stare. The engine of their sedan idled for fully an hour before they could even speak.

END

GYPSIES

*D*ej, Romania...

There was the smell of ashes and smoldering spices in the cramped space. Mirella, leaning over a small trunk, placed cards face up on a black, cotton cloth spread across the top. Her eyes strained to see the images on the cards illuminated only by candlelight.

"H-m-m... that's interesting," she mumbled to herself, then carefully placed the next card. Tapping the card after seeing what it was, she nodded saying, "Good... good." Her concentration was broken by the calling of her name.

"Mirella, Mirella," a voice bellowed.

"I'm in here, Boldo. In the vardo."

Behind her, a piece of dingy canvas moved, and then a head poked into the wagon's interior. Dark eyes quickly scanned the scene. "Woman, you need to get the fire going. Everyone is awakening and they will be hungry. You can play with your cards later."

"Boldo, we will be getting visitors soon," she said over her shoulder, then flipped another card.

"Is it the authorities?"

She couldn't see his face, but she heard the concern in his voice. "No dear, they are foreigners. Coming from across the ocean. I'm getting a sense of wealth from the cards. It's a good sign."

She was about to go to the next card when he touched her shoulder. "Later, Mirella. You need to gather the firewood and get things ready for the clan." He was firm in his request and then left.

The old woman gathered her cards, and folded the black cloth. She placed them neatly into the trunk. Blowing out the candle, she followed after her husband. The vardo rocked and creaked as she stepped down from it.

As the men, women, and children gathered around the morning fire, Boldo Mirga, the head of his clan announced to the family, "It is time we leave this place and move on. Let us make plans."

"Brother, where are we headed?"

"There is a festival starting in Transylvania, Yanko. It will give us an opportunity to make some money. Mirella and your wife, Florica, can read the tarot cards and palms. Your daughters, Luminitsa and Femi, will dance as we play our pan flutes. Our sons, Marko and Tobar have shown their skills in pick-pocketing and will work their way through the crowd that comes to see and hear us. Mirella has shared with me we are going to have some special visitors from afar, and they are of wealth. We will soon see what they are willing to share with us."

"*Or take it*," Yanko declared with gusto to the approval most of the clan.

Yanko's wife did not share his sentiment and sat with a solemn look.

Seeing her mood, Boldo questioned her. "Florica, you seem to have something on your mind. What is it?"

She hesitated, then said, "I saw seagulls flying over the vardo yesterday. It is a bad omen about these visitors."

Her son, Tobar, elbowed his cousin, Marko, in the rib. "Tell them what *we* have seen."

Marko, somewhat shy, looked to his father and said, "We saw a falling star a few nights ago, and Yanko was hit with bird droppings this morning when we were cleaning ourselves by the creek."

"Were they seagull droppings?" mused Luminitsa, the older of the two girls.

"Enough!" shouted Boldo, waving an arm. "Mirella saw the cards and there was nothing to indicate any evil befalling our clan. The seagulls you saw may be an indication of a bad omen, but that only spells trouble for those foreigners. I don't want to hear any more about omens."

He clapped his hands. "Now everyone, go ready yourselves, we break camp soon."

As the members scurried off to prepare for their travel, Mirella touched the arm of her husband. "I wasn't able to complete reading the tarot cards, Boldo. You needed me to make the fire, remember? What if I just didn't determine the outcome of the visit by these strangers?"

"Well, you can try and read the cards again. But right now, we need to gather our things. It will take two days to get to Transylvania, so we need to leave now."

Somewhere outside Denver, Colorado...

"Sin, have you located our passports?"

"Yes dear, I put them in the zipper part of my carry-on luggage. How are you coming on your packing?" he asked, eyeing the pile of clothes on the bed.

"I can't find a dress I want to take with me. It's that black knee-length one with the spaghetti straps that I bought last week." She continued rummaging through her closet.

"I'm sure you'll find it, Claire. It's getting dark. Are you coming with me?"

"No Sin, I'm quite content, and I have lots of things to get ready before we leave on our trip. You go quench your thirst, dear. I know how you get before a big journey."

"Suit yourself, dear. I won't be long. I just need that pick-me-up if you know what I mean." He winked as he departed the bedroom.

Shortly, she heard the front door close, paused from her activities, and moved to the open window. The evening air flowed gently into the room through the screened opening. Her eyes glimpsed the near half-moon before they fell on the figure below. "I love you, Sinclair," she yelled.

He turned and waved acknowledging that he heard her, then got into the BMW.

When his vehicle disappeared through the property gates, she returned to her closet. "There you are," she said, pulling out a black dress. She took off her clothes and slipped the dress on to measure its fit.

Then, she went into the bathroom and rummaged through her make-up carrier. Pulling out a tube of lipstick, she spread a coating of the red wax across her lips. The blood-red color contrasted sharply with her fair skin, long dark hair, and black dress. "I love this color," she said, pursing her lips to simulate a kiss to the image reflected in the mirror.

While his wife finished her packing, Sinclair soon pulled into a parking lot in front of a bright neon sign that read: *Wild Country*. He remained in his vehicle keenly watching as men and women, wearing their finest cowboy hats and boots, entered the establishment. The neon beer signs in the windows and the music blaring out the front door signaled he had arrived at the right place to satisfy his thirst.

#

"I didn't hear you come in last night," said Claire, putting the last of her things into a suitcase.

"Yeah, I stayed later than I thought I would," he answered.

"Where did you go?"

He hefted her closed bag from the bed and stood it on the floor. "That country and western bar the next town over. There was a good crowd there."

"Did you meet anyone?"

The look on his face told her the whole story. "I hope you were careful," she said, poking his shoulder.

"You have nothing to worry about, Claire," he said, grabbing her around the waste. "We are bound together forever." He gave her a kiss of assurance, then added, "I quenched my craving and came straight home."

"Alright then, but I'm ready to go." She pushed him away and took a last look around the room. "We need to get to the airport by ten o'clock. Going through security could take a while. It's bad enough we have to layover in New York tonight, but there's only one daily flight that goes directly to Bucharest."

"Lead the way, dear. I'm anxious to get started."

Bucharest, Romania...

Claire Robertson looked out the portal of the descending aircraft. "I didn't think Bucharest would be as spread out as it looks from up here," she said to her husband. Did you know how big the city was?"

Not hearing a reply, she looked over to Sinclair. "Are you alright? You look paler than usual."

He shifted uncomfortably in his seat. "You would think with all the flying I do that I would be used to this."

"That's because you're usually doing the flying yourself, dear. You're just not used to having others fly you." She giggled. "We'll be on the ground soon." Her attention returned to the portal. "Did your mother ever talk much about Bucharest or Romania?"

"No. I only know our ancestry goes back to the Transylvania area. If I remember, she said the family name was Holomeck. She never was into her family history. I'm third generation to the United States, so it has been quite a while since my mother's family moved there."

"Still, it's exciting to be here now, isn't it? You might be able to discover more about your ancestry."

"I hope so," he said, grabbing the arms of his seat as they descended. "That's one of the reasons I wanted to come here."

A short while later, Sinclair and Claire Robertson cleared customs and caught a shuttle to the rental car rental facility. Leaving there in a dark-colored, luxury vehicle, they headed for the airport exit indicated by the vehicle's GPS in the direction of Transylvania.

Claire took out her I-phone and did an internet search of Romania. She went to the events section of the travel site. "We're in luck, Sin. There is a festival in Transylvania this whole week. I'm sure there will be lots of people and excitement, so we're sure to get our fill of everything we need to sustain a good trip."

"That's great, Claire. I'm sure you're as ready as I am to rejuvenate ourselves when we get there."

"I admit I have begun to feel out-of-sorts," she added, "but the festival is just the thing I need to bring back my vitality."

She spent the better part of the next hour searching topics and texting to her friends back home.

"What's this?" she unconsciously said to her husband.

"What's what?

"One of my girlfriends texted a young woman's body was found this morning in a wooded area near *Wild Country*. The police are saying it appears to be a homicide, but they aren't saying much more pending an autopsy." Claire then added her own commentary, "It doesn't appear as if the person who committed the crime was careful?" She looked over at Sinclair with raised eyebrows.

Outside Transylvania...

The Mirga clan had completed setting up their encampment in a wooded clearing a few miles from the location of the festival. Boldo gave orders for the women to begin their preparations for the evening meal by gathering firewood.

"I am going to ride into Transylvania," announced Boldo as he saddled the horse that pulled his vardo, "and speak to the people in charge of the festival about our participation. Yanko, will stay here and look after everyone while I'm gone. Marko and Tobar, you fetch water from the creek near here and fill the barrel. I should be back before it gets dark." He mounted the horse and rode off at a trot toward the city.

As he approached the festival area, riding along the shoulder of the road, a dark-colored, luxury sedan passed him. Claire's head turned to look at the horse-mounted man. "What a beautiful saddle," she remarked.

"I can't say much for the horse," Sinclair added, looking past her at the scene. "I'll bet he's a gypsy."

"What makes you say that?"

"I don't know, his overall look I guess. Reminds me of pictures I saw on the internet. This part of the world is full of gypsy clans and families. I'm sure we're going to see lots of them before our trip is over."

"I hope I get to know one personally. I find the thought of a gypsy very intriguing," Claire said, keeping her eyes on the rider now behind them.

Sinclair gave a hearty laugh as he continued on into Transylvania. "Your thirst for the unexpected is refreshing, Claire. I hope you get your wish."

Boldo unconsciously watched the car move along the road in front of him. A short while later, he arrived at the outskirts of the city where the festival was being held. After questioning a few workers, he located the tent that housed the event organizers and went inside. Being directed to the person in charge, he introduced himself.

"My name is Boldo Mirga. My family and I are travelling south. We learned about your festival and I was wondering if we could participate. My wife reads tarot cards and my brother's wife is a palm reader. We won't be any trouble and we could use the money."

The man looked Boldo over. "We already have another gypsy group here that will be reading the crystal. I'm not sure we need other fortune tellers."

Boldo was persistent. "The festival appears large enough to accommodate one more gypsy clan," he said "Plus, we also bring music and dance. I'm sure the visitors would enjoy that. We are a very colorful group, and as I said, we won't be any trouble."

The man hesitated. "Alright, but there is a fee to work the festival for each day you're here, and I don't want you to set up near the other clan. Come with me, I'll show you where you can establish your tent."

Boldo followed him, and after making the necessary agreements, headed back to his encampment.

Hotel in Transylvania...

"Claire? Would you be partial to exploring the town?"

"It's already getting dark, dear. Maybe we should have dinner first. I'm feeling a little weak and I think a good meal would help me immensely."

"You may be right. "I'm getting a little hungry myself."

"Do you think we're safe here at night. I mean, what about vampire bats," she teased.

Sinclair gave a laugh. "Claire, you know that's all just tales don't you. There *are* bats in Romania, but vampire bats are only found in the Americas. I'm sure we'll be quite safe."

Her eyes glistened as she looked into his. "Okay Sin, but still, it's a creepy thought, don't you think?"

"Yes. That would be creepy. Now, I'm ready to go if you're ready."

"Let's go," she said, pulling on his arm.

Outside in the evening sky two, small-winged mammals hovered over the city.

Mirga Encampment Outside Transylvania...

The next morning, Mirella left the vardo as Boldo readied himself for the day. She found her son, Marko sleeping under the wagon and went to wake him. Putting a hand on his shoulder, she gently shook him. He rolled to his other side in response and stayed silent. It was then she noticed a thin trail of dried blood that began a few inches below his right ear and disappeared into the collar of his shirt. Suddenly, the unmistakable hoot of an owl startled her even more. Panicked, she shook Marko until he gained his full consciousness. Temporarily relieved, she sent him to wash himself and then went back to her husband.

"Did you hear the owl?" she asked him more than concerned.

"I did. Is that what has you so rattled?" Boldo asked seeing her expression.

"It is another bad omen, Boldo. First, the sighting of seagulls by Florica, and now this. You know what it means, Boldo... when an owl hoots closely after dawn. It is said that the bird is calling a soul from a human body and is considered a threat of death to the family. "

"Gypsy nonsense, Mirella," her husband chided. "We live in the twenty-first century now. Don't be given to old tales that were meant to scare children."

"I saw blood on Marko's neck when I woke him. I sent him to wash."

"The boy is very active... he probably got nicked by a tree branch." Irritation continued to mark his words. "We have to be going soon to the festival. I'll check Marko, then I'm going to hook the horse to the vardo. Get yourself ready.... we leave within the hour."

As he disappeared from inside the wagon, Mirella glanced at her trunk. Knowing there was no time for her to read the tarot cards, she gave up the idea and put on her most colorful outfit.

On Boldo's schedule, the clan departed in one wagon leaving his brother's vardo and a partially dismantled camp behind and set out for the festival grounds.

Hotel in Transylvania...

Waking in their hotel room, Sinclair and Claire stretched their limbs to shake off the stiffness from their sleep.

"Goodness, what time is it?" asked Claire, looking at the light peeking through the curtain.

Sinclair glanced at the bedside clock. "Relax, hon. It's only a little after ten. We were out later than we planned. Did you sleep well, dear?"

"Oh yes. You know I always sleep better on a full stomach. But we shouldn't have been out that late, Sin. Especially in a strange environment. The only thing that kept me from being more nervous was the half-moon that illuminated into the shadows."

"You know I wouldn't let anything happen to you, Claire," Sinclair reassured while touching her hand.

"I know dear, but we don't know this country, and tourists are always an easy target."

"If it will make you feel better, we'll spend the day at the festival and stay in tonight. Tomorrow though, I'd enjoy a visit to Bran Castle, popularly known as Dracula's Castle. We couldn't come here and not visit it. Then, we'll leave to visit the town where my mother's family is from."

"Sounds like a plan," she agreed, "but right now, I get first dibs on the bathroom."

"Go ahead, dear. I'm not ready to get up yet. I'll lie here and check the local news for a weather report."

Festival, Transylvania...

"Yanko, my son is not feeling well today... the boy is tired. Could you tell Tobar to unhook the horse and tie him to the wagon. I'll keep my saddle nearby so one of us can return to the camp later and check on our belongings there. I believe the encampment is well hidden in the trees, but it's best not to take chances."

"Alright, Boldo. I'll see that Tobar takes care of it, but he's anxious to work the crowd. He already lifted this bracelet from a tourist." He held up a gold band that caught the glint of the sun. "It's fourteen karats."

"Very good. Whatever we get from the visitors will help to make up for the fees we have to pay to be here. I don't know if Marko will be steady enough to help today, so I want him to rest in the vardo. When you return, Luminitsa and Femi will be ready to dance to the music of our pan flutes. The crowd is beginning to grow, and we need to pull them over to us by entertaining them."

Yanko grinned wide, nodded, and set out to locate Tobar.

Within a short span of time, the sound of flutes filled the air. Luminitsa and Femi, adorned in their brightest dresses, performed traditional Romani dances. Their bare feet keeping perfect time to the music so skillfully played by Boldo and Yanko. The girls waved their skirts beautifully for the people that gathered to watch them, always mindful of the coins being tossed into a nearby basket.

Their wild display of entertainment quickly caught the eye and ear of festival guests and soon mesmerized the crowd that gathered around them.

"Look Sin, those girls over there are so cute. Look how they dance. Let's go over and watch them," said Claire, pulling on his arm.

He joyfully followed her. They watched until the music stopped.

Boldo stepped forward and thanked the crowd for their generosity and invited them to have their palms read or a reading of the tarot cards while the girls took a rest.

A few people stepped closer to the tents where Mirella and Florica sat waiting to show their skills. They dared one another to have a reading.

"Sin, do you recognize that man who made the announcement?" Claire asked, pointing to the dark-skinned announcer.

"Yeah, he's the rider we saw along the road. See I told you he was a gypsy."

"And there's his horse and saddle over by the wagon. They make a cute group don't they?" She didn't wait for his answer before pulling on him again. "I want to have a tarot reading. I've never had my fortune told."

"Do you think that wise, Claire? What if… "

"Come on, it will be fun."

The hairs stood on the back of Mirella's neck when she saw the couple approach. Nonetheless, she invited Claire to sit across the table from her and began to deal the cards. The sixth card she laid out caught Claire's attention. It was an image of a cloaked woman kneeling in front of a barren bush. In one hand was a scythe. Mirella caught her breath.

"What does *that* card mean?" asked Claire, pointing to it. "From your reaction, I take it it's not good."

Mirella was speechless. She continued to stare at the card in front of her.

Sinclair, standing next to his wife, leaned over the table and put a finger on the card. "My wife asked you what this card means?"

Mirella looked into his eyes, and then into Claire's eyes. Not intending to say anything she blurted out, "It is a death card. You, or someone you know is going to die!"

Claire gave an uncomfortable chuckle. "This is all play isn't it? I mean, tarot cards don't really tell the future, do they?"

"Maybe I made a mistake," she said, picking up the cards and reshuffling them. "Let me try again." She began to lay them one by one. Two of the first five cards were different than the first time she placed them. But the sixth card was again the death card.

"*Sinclair, what just happened,*" she said frightened, then stood and moved away from the table to her husband.

He reached for her and held her tight attempting to console her from the shock of the words spoken by the gypsy woman. "It's alright, dear... this is all fake anyway. We must go."

He led his wife away without paying for the reading.

Boldo had witnessed the entire event and moved to his wife. "Why did you display the death card? You know that always sends them away without paying?"

"I-I didn't intend for it to come up," she stammered. I even put it on the bottom of the deck when I reshuffled them."

"It's just as well. With all their concern over the card, they didn't notice Tobar taking the man's wallet. I saw Tobar go behind the vardo and give it to Yanko. We have to hide it in case the man realizes it's gone and reports us to the authorities."

He could see his wife was distressed. "Get yourself under control, Mirella. You have more readings to perform."

Boldo watched the Robertson's gain distance as they moved away across the fairgrounds, and then joined his brother and Tobar behind the wagon.

Holding out a stack of money Yanko said, "Brother, this guy is loaded. Look at all these large bills. And, there are several credit cards here as well."

"Forget the credit cards," Boldo insisted. "When the man realizes his wallet is lost, he'll notify the card companies. We have to get the things Tobar stole away from this place. Take the horse back to our encampment and make sure everything is alright there. Hide all the valuables we have collected… we have enough for today."

"Okay, brother. I will return as soon as I can." He saddled the horse, and directed it toward their camp.

#

On the far side of the festival grounds, Claire turned to her husband. "How was my act? Convincing?"

"It sure was, Claire. I think you really got to that gypsy woman. She was completely stunned by your reaction. *Death card... now there's a good one.*" He laughed out loud and she joined in.

"You know what is really funny?"

"You mean more funny than the look on that gypsy woman's face?" she asked, still giggling.

He patted his back pocket. "They thought they were slick and lifted my wallet. I sensed a young boy moving behind me, but he was very good. I barely felt a thing when he removed it. Then I saw him go behind the wagon and meet another man."

"*Sin*, that had all our money and credit cards in it. We have to go tell the police."

"Not necessary, Claire. You wait here, and I'll be back in a few minutes." He left her standing in the shade of a tree with a puzzled look on her face.

Ten minutes later, he returned and whispered something into her ear. She grinned and nodded as they headed back to their hotel.

Mirga Encampment Outside Transylvania...

Yanko reached the encampment within thirty minutes and tied his horse to his vardo. Everything looked just as it had when the group left that morning. Looking around for a place to hide the stolen property, he noticed a large, dead log with a hollow in it at the edge of the clearing. *No one will find these things in there,* he thought, and then started to move toward it. Suddenly, he heard the flutter of small wings and then a voice over his shoulder.

"I'll take my wallet back if you please."

He turned his head to see the Robertson's standing in a position behind him. A shiver ran through Yanko's spine.

Turning to face them, "H-how did you find me? H-how did you get here so fast?" Yanko moaned in disbelief.

"We were here last night. And, when you're a vampire, you get around pretty easy."

"*M-u-l-l-o!*" Yanko screamed, holding his hands out in front of him. "B-but vampires can't be out in the light of day!"

"That's old school thinking," said Sinclair. "We have evolved over the centuries. We even see our reflection in mirrors now. It must be from the changes in everyone's bloodline," he said, turning to Claire. "Don't you agree, dear?"

Yanko dropped his sack of stolen artifacts and ran to his wagon. Reaching in, he grabbed a shotgun and aimed it at the Robertson's. He pulled the trigger sending up a cloud of smoke that temporarily obscured his vision.

When the smoke cleared, two, small-winged mammals attacked him. The first one attacked his neck making him drop the shotgun when he reached to remove it. The second landed with its feet in his eyes blinding him.

Yanko dropped to his knees, and put his hands to his bleeding face. Through his agony he again heard Sinclair's voice.

"You'll feel a sharp jab in your neck, followed by a warm feeling. I'd advise you not to fight it." There was a brief pause, "Ladies first, my dear."

Hotel in Transylvania...

"I'm quite looking forward to seeing Bran Castle tomorrow, Claire. How about you?" Sinclair yelled into the next room.

Claire spread lipstick across her lips while looking at her reflection in the bathroom mirror. Then she responded. "I hope while there, we get to meet more gypsies. I can still taste the sweetness of their blood."

She licked her blood-red lips.

END

HALFWAY TO
MAY 18th

Ted sat across from a magazine reporter. The meeting had been scheduled the previous week based on a call from the magazine's headquarters in New York City. As Ted understood it, they were planning on publishing a number of articles about lottery winners from across the country.

The magazine had initially contacted Ted's parents about doing an interview for a piece they were writing about his sister, Melissa. But his parents were adamant that they were not interested, and even warned Ted not to become involved. But there he was, sitting before an eager ear, and ready to talk about his sister.

"Mr. Rosen, do you mind if I make a recording of our conversation?"

"No, that will be fine."

Ted heard a faint beep before the recorder was placed between them.

"I'll ask you a few questions, but please feel free to say as much as you want, Mr. Rosen. We'll edit what we record down to those parts we believe our readers will want to know. Are you ready?"

"Yes."

"I first want to ask for the record, are you aware our conversation is being recorded, and do you give us permission to use any statements you make to our magazine?"

"Yes, I agree to have this interview recorded."

"Tell me when your sister's story began." The interviewer leaned back, waiting for Ted to respond.

"My parents would tell you it all started on March tenth, which is the date halfway between New Year's Day and May eighteenth. March tenth being the day my sister, Melissa, found the lottery ticket. However, one could make the case the story really began before then, when my sister drove to St. Louis to attend an antiques appraisal event being held there. I happened to be visiting my parents one day in February, when my sister called them excited about what she was told by one of the appraisers regarding an old rug she found several years before."

The interviewer pushed the recorder closer to Ted. "Sorry for the interruption, please continue."

"Melissa told us that she found the rug in a dumpster, along with several other items that could be re-used, or adapted into something else. She thought the rug was an Indian weave, but the expert told her it was actually a tribal rug woven in Persia by nomads. He also said he could date the rug by the uses of the dyes, mentioning that one dye in particular, that makes the color purple, is no longer used. She described to us how he folded over a beige section of the rug revealing a purple color at the root of the knot, which confirmed the rug could be dated back to the eighteen sixties. As the rug was in remarkable condition, he said it was worth about four thousand dollars at auction. Of course, we were stunned by what she told us, and happy for her good fortune."

Ted paused. "But I know Melissa's journey started long before then."

"Please tell our readers, Mr. Rosen."

"When she was a freshman in high school, Melissa developed a fascination with trash cans and dumpsters. You see, my sister was a recycler of things long before 'recycling' developed into a household trend. At an early age, she would go out the night before the neighborhood trash was to be picked up, and rummage through the cans sitting in the alleyway. I thought it was disgusting, that is, until she brought me the coolest toy truck. Anyway, her diving turned out to be the talk and taunt of the other kids at our school. She didn't care though; she once said, "they'll be laughing out the other side of their faces when I find something valuable."

"After a time, she stopped diving hoping that the teasing would stop. She never told me directly why, but I think the new boy who came to our school late that schoolyear had something to do with it. I don't believe it was coincidence that he became her first boyfriend when the next fall term began. By then, the other kids had moved on to teasing someone else. I was just glad it wasn't me."

"Melissa managed to stay away from people's trash for a long time. But then, in her senior year of high school, there was that dramatic breakup. Her boyfriend dumped her for the homecoming queen. It was enough to send her over the edge, and she started diving again."

"A year or two later, when my sister was in college, she fell in with a group of what I referred to as 'tree-huggers'. You know, those peace-loving, do-gooders that only eat plants, and rail against all forms of greed and waste. Anyway, she shacked up with two other girls, and I swear to this day that every possession they had, came from a dumpster. Including their clothes."

The interviewer changed the subject. "What studies did your sister pursue?"

"Much to the chagrin of our parents, Melissa was a candidate for a sociology degree. They wanted her to go into law or the medical field, to which she seemed fully capable of doing. But her answer to them was always the same, sociology develops one's appreciation of diversity, as well as, a knowledge base about human behavior, social organization, and culture. She felt strongly about one day being able to help change some of society's anti-social practices, which she believed was just as important as healing someone or keeping them from jail."

Ted casually shifted in his chair, then continued. "I once read an article that said sociology was the preferred study of those who don't necessarily follow the crowd, but are fascinated by other's behavior. That statement, succinctly described my sister... she definitely marched to the beat of her own drum."

"Do you mind if I have a drink?" Ted asked, pointing to a tray of bottled water.

The interviewer passed him one of the plastic bottles.

Ted opened it and took a good swallow of the liquid before continuing.

"After Melissa graduated, she moved to Springfield, Illinois and converted into an activist for the Young Women's Empowerment Project. One time, she chained herself to the legs of the statue of Abe Lincoln in front of the capitol building in protest of the state not adequately funding drug rehabilitation programs. Anyway, she continued dumpster diving, but to my knowledge she never found anything valuable until that fateful day on March 10th."

"What did she find, Mr. Rosen?"

"Melissa found a plastic bag filled with used lottery tickets in a trash bin behind the local grocery store. You know, the ones people throw away after they check them on the reader. For a week, she took handfuls of tickets and re-scanned them at machines around town. I think she told me it was on the fourth day that she discovered one of the tickets was a winner."

"Really?" said the interviewer. "But if the tickets were already scanned by someone else, how did she explain the previous owner didn't turn it in?"

"*She* called it fate… there were two tickets that sort of stuck together, and she believed the previous owner only scanned the top ticket before discarding them."

"Your sister must have been really excited when the clerk told her she won the two point seven-million-dollar prize," said the magazine rep.

"Oh yeah! You better believe it. She was shaking so bad, she could barely fill out the paperwork. The clerk told her it would take about eight weeks to receive her check."

"Had your sister ever been lucky like that before?"

"With the exception of finding that rug, never. But after finding that ticket, all sorts of lucky things happened to her."

"Oh, Mr. Rosen… like what?"

Two weeks after that, she was notified she won a washer and dryer for entering a magazine contest. Then, there was the weekend trip she took with some friends to Las Vegas to celebrate the lottery win. While there, she hit for six thousand dollars on one of the slot machines. Even came back with most of it. But it didn't stop there. She was the tenth caller on a morning talk show and won opening day tickets to a Cardinals game with seats behind home plate. Yeah, everything was going her way until the day she went to the lottery office to pick up her check."

The interviewer leaned in toward Ted. "She didn't have to go far to get it, did she? I mean the Illinois lottery's central office is located right there in Springfield, right?"

"That's correct. It's in the Willard Ice Building on West Jefferson Street."

"And the date she went to pick up her winnings was May eighteenth, right?"

"Yes."

"So, tell the readers what happened."

Ted cleared his throat, then took another drink of water.

"On the day before, Melissa received a call from the lottery office to come in and pick up the check. She was reminded to bring in a number of identification documents, and that she should dress appropriately because her picture would be taken holding a giant check facsimile. The next day, May eighteenth, Melissa sent me a text when she arrived at the parking lot: *Only minutes from picking up my winnings. So excited. Will call you afterward.*"

"But she never got the chance, did she?"

Ted replied calmly. "No. Her lucky streak suddenly ended."

"What do you mean?"

"Melissa was killed before she left the parking lot. Police informed my parents it was a random act of violence carried out by a stranger. They said the person who pulled the trigger was likely hallucinating from the drug, LSD, found in a later blood test, and there was no telling what that person was thinking at the time of their altered state."

"That is one heck of a story, Mr. Rosen. Your sister was the winner of a substantial lottery win, but never had the chance to collect it. What happens with the money now?"

"It was officially claimed when she signed the back of the ticket and filled out the lottery's paperwork. But it will be tied up in court for a while. My parents believe our family is entitled to the win. However, my sister had a will and the only beneficiary she listed was the National Institute on Drug Abuse. So I don't think I, or my parents, have a valid claim."

"How does that make you feel, Mr. Rosen?"

"As far as I'm concerned, it is a fitting ending to the story, but I still haven't wrapped my head around the irony of it all."

On the one-year anniversary of his sister's death, Ted received an advance copy of the magazine containing the article written about his sister titled, *Halfway to May 18th*. After reading the article, he thought it only fitting he purchase a lottery ticket in her memory from the same grocery store where she had found her winning lottery ticket.

When he arrived at the store, police squad cars were arriving in numbers and positioning themselves near all exits of the building. Small bands of shoppers were being ushered across the street and away from the designated danger zone by uniformed officers.

Ted maneuvered his way to one of the groups, which had a good view of the grocer's front doors, and asked a woman what was happening.

"It was freaky," she said, shaking. "I was checking out my groceries when this crazed man pulled a gun on a clerk a few aisles behind me, and started yelling nonsense. Shoppers started running in all directions. I just got the hell out of there. I think he was on drugs."

Ted subsequently worked his way as far forward of the crowd as he could to get a better view of the action. He positioned himself behind a woman, who from the back, reminded him of his sister, and peered over her shoulder at the scene across the street.

Without warning, the armed gunman stormed out of the front door and began firing.

Police immediately returned fire with several bullets striking the man. But before the gunman went down, he was able to get off a final shot.

The woman that Ted previously talked to screamed behind him.

The next day, the lead story of the local newspaper read: *May 18th is a day that will long be remembered by this community. In a shootout with police, a gunman, who police believed was strung out on LSD, killed an innocent bystander in a crowd of people that gathered to watch the incident unfold. What makes the story so bizarre is that, Melissa Rosen, a person previously thought deceased, was killed by a stray bullet seemingly fired from the gunman's weapon. Her brother, Ted Rosen, who caught her as she fell, was later taken for psychiatric observation following the incident, and....*

END

NORSE COFFER

Charlotte unwrapped the band aid and stuck it to the wound on her right forearm. She didn't know how the cut occurred, but she was able to stem the flow of bleeding by applying direct pressure on it with a gauze pad. The last thing she remembered was heading into her aunt's bedroom. But what happened when she arrived there was a complete mystery. She doctored the wound and went downstairs.

"Did you bring my necklace with you, Char?" asked her aunt, primping her hair in front of the hall mirror.

"Necklace ...? No, I forgot to get it."

Her aunt noticed her fiddling with the band aid.

"What happened, dearie?" she said, taking the girl's arm for a closer inspection. The top of the band aid was spotted with a dull, red color.

"I'm not sure. One minute I went into your bedroom to get your necklace, and the next I was blotting a cut on my arm."

Her aunt gave her a look of displeasure.

"I'm sorry, auntie," she said, noticing her expression. "I'll go back and get it for you."

Aunt Unni's face softened. She grabbed at Charlotte's shoulder to stay her. "That's alright, dear. I don't really need it with this blouse anyway. And, I'm not mad at you," she assured. "Seeing your wound, made something else cross my mind. Now, you run along, and I'll see you tonight."

"Are you sure, auntie? It will only take me a second to go get it."

Her aunt shooed her toward the door, grabbing a sweater and an umbrella from nearby as they moved in that direction.

"Take these," she offered. "They are calling for rain this afternoon and it may be a little chilly. Would you mind picking up milk and bread on your way home?" her aunt asked, untucking her niece's long, red hair from the sweater as Charlotte slipped it on.

Nodding that she would, Charlotte gave Unni a kiss on the cheek and then headed out.

With her ward departed, Aunt Unni's gaze turned to the stair landing above. She began to slowly ascend the steps, uncertain if she wanted to confirm her suspicions.

Reaching her dresser, she pulled open the top drawer. Observing an ornately-carved, wooden box had been shifted, she gasped, then yelled, "*Fenrir!*" The words were spoken not as a surprise, but more of chastisement.

She spoke again. "You're being bad, Fenrir. We can't have that... not yet." Her finger stroked a geometric shape carved into the top of the box. The digit's nerve endings feeling a knotted, interlaced pattern, and her eyes reflecting the zoomorphic shape of an antlered stag in the design.

"Soon enough," she muttered, picking up the box.

She stepped toward her closet and opened the door. Placing the box on a shelf just above her head, she covered it with a pile of folded sweaters. "I know you were only playing, Fenrir, but Charlotte isn't ready for such things."

#

Later that evening, Charlotte sat at the dinner table with her aunt and remarked, "It was quiet in the bookstore today."

With eyes shimmering from the reflected light overhead, her aunt looked at her ward replying, "Did you use your time well, dear?"

"Yes, I finally vacuumed the dust from the top rows of books. You know, the ones that never get touched. Then I rearranged them alphabetically by author. When I was done, I noticed the rows looked similar to notes on a musical staff. I found myself humming a tune."

Unni leaned toward her niece; excitement in her voice. "And did anything else happen?"

"No. A customer came into the store turning away my attention."

Unni's posture reverted to a relaxed state. "Could you pass me the bread, please."

One month later…

"I remember you!" Charlotte exclaimed, and quickly blushed from her outburst.

Staring at a young man on the other side of the counter, she added, "I'm sorry. I didn't mean to be so bold."

"I remember you too," he automatically responded. "You were humming a melody when I came in. I thought I recognized it, but you stopped before I could place it. Do you know what the name of that piece was?"

"Sorry, but I don't," she responded. "I find myself humming when I arrange the books on the shelves. Curious isn't it?" Then she offered holding out her hand, "I'm Charlotte."

"Arnold. Arnold Hunt. My friends call me Arnie," he said, shaking her hand.

She immediately felt something strange in his grip. "Is that the name you were born with?"

He looked at her inquisitively. "No... my birth certificate has Arnbjorg on it. But I had it legally changed to Arnold when I grew old enough. It's easier to pronounce."

Charlotte chuckled. "Did you know Arnbjorg is an old Icelandic name? It's derived from 'arn' meaning eagle and 'bjorg' meaning save or rescue. Are you here to rescue me, Mr. Hunt?"

"Not that I'm aware of. Do you need rescuing, Charlotte?"

Her response was a laugh.

"How did you know the meaning of my name?" he quizzed.

She glanced around the room, then back to him. "I read a lot, and have a good sense about people. Would you be interested to know what else I observed about you?"

"I'm afraid to ask," he said.

"You abbreviated Arnold to Arnie. That's a term used to describe someone of great strength; someone with the ability to leap tall buildings and pound tanks into trash cans."

He stood back from the counter and unbuttoned his coat to reveal a slim body. "I'm a mathematics teacher. Do I resemble a superhero?"

Charlotte laughed again. "I don't know… I hear good things come in small packages."

"You seem to know quite a bit about old Norse names," he remarked.

"My roots are Scandinavian. I live with my aunt who is named, Unni. She is very instructional about my heritage."

"But Charlotte isn't Scandinavian," he said.

"That was the name given to me. But I admit, it is fairly unremarkable."

"And what is your last name?" he added.

"Oh it's very mysterious, Mr. Hunt. It's Martin... Charlotte Martin. But my mother's maiden name was Steenberg. The same surname as my aunt."

"Pleased to meet you Miss Martin. Uh, it is Miss, isn't it?"

"Yes. Now that we have that out of the way, how may I help you?"

He looked around the book shop. "Most of these books look to be rare or outdated copies. What I'm looking for is newer. I think written in the 1980's. I don't remember the name, but it has to do with mathematics and the concept of time travel. Does that ring a bell with you?"

The girl thought for a minute. "No, can't say that it does. But I don't know every book in here either. I'll keep an eye out for it."

"Thank you, Charlotte."

He turned to leave.

"How do I get in touch with you if I do find it?"

"Call the middle school, and ask for me. I teach math there. See you around, Miss Martin."

In a flash he was gone.

"How was work today?" asked Aunt Unni across the dinner table.

"Uneventful. I only sold eight books. I don't know how that store stays open."

"It has been there a long time, dear. I'm fairly certain that the owner owns the building and probably picks the books up from garage sales or from thrift stores to resell them."

"I met a teacher from the middle school," Charlotte said. "He came in looking for a book, but I'm sure we don't have it."

The word 'he' caught Unni's attention. "Describe him to me?"

"Kind of plain. Sort of handsome, but not overly so. He fits the image of what one would think of as a mathematics teacher."

Her aunt leaned in. "Did he flirt with you?"

"Oh auntie, heavens no. He's just a nice man looking for a book. It's only the second time I've seen him."

"You're a pretty girl, Charlotte. I don't know why a man wouldn't be taken with you. But I'm glad there's nothing serious there. You're too young to get involved that way. You have plenty of time to meet the man of your dreams." Unni paused. "Pass me the milk, please."

#

A low voice growled. "Mother, when are you going to release me?"

"It is not time yet, my darling Fenrir," she said, taking the box from her shelf closet. "But the time is nigh for you to take your revenge. I, your mother, Angrboda, will set you free on the night of the dark moon."

There was a knock on Unni's bedroom door. She quickly returned the box to the closet shelf and re-covered it with sweaters. "Come in, my dear," she invited.

"I thought I heard voices," said Charlotte, entering and looking around the room.

Her aunt closed the closet door. "It's just the talk of an old woman who can't remember where she puts things, dear. Nothing to worry about."

A shiver caused Charlotte to look beyond Unni at the door behind her. "I feel as if there is another presence here, auntie. I am getting a strong sense of it coming from your closet."

Unni grabbed her niece's arm and pulled her to the bed. "Sit, dear, and tell me what you perceive."

"I'm not quite sure, auntie. I find the feeling hard to describe. It's as though I am being summoned in some way." She unknowingly grabbed at the scar on her right forearm, which did not go unnoticed by her aunt.

Unni stroked her red hair. "Women in our family have been known to have a sixth sense. Your mother was particularly susceptive to visions. Perhaps you are beginning to acquire her abilities."

"Have *you* ever had them?"

Her aunt hesitated. "I haven't had the experience, but I know it exists. Close your eyes and tell me what you see."

The girl closed her eyes. "... I see the image of a giant wolf. The wolf is bound by strong bonds, but is straining to free itself."

Charlotte could not see the half-grin that stretched the wrinkles around her aunt's mouth. "What else, dear? What do you see?"

"Nothing. The image is gone." She opened her eyes. "I'm frightened, auntie."

"There, there. Let me give you a hug." Unni embraced her niece.

"What could it mean?" Charlotte asked, pushing her to arm's length and looking into her aunt's face.

"It's probably just an overactive imagination. Have you read any books about wolves recently? You tell me that you are always reading something when your workday slows. I'm sure it is nothing, dear."

"No, I haven't read anything that has animals in it," she confirmed. "I'm especially sure that I haven't browsed selections that would give me *that* kind of an image."

"Well then, you have nothing to worry about. Let's go downstairs, dear. I'll fix you something to eat."

She pulled Charlotte from the bed and led her out of the room.

###

Later that evening, as Unni prepared for bed...

"Mother, the girl is getting stronger, isn't she?" growled a low voice.

"Yes, Fenrir. She sensed you. Soon, you won't be able to put her under your spell as you did last month when you had her cut her forearm."

"Then release me now, mother, so that I may *taste* her blood."

"Now Fenrir, you took too much of a chance last month. If she would have opened the box before it is time, you would not be able to vanquish the heroes."

The low, growling voice answered. "I have been prisoner for centuries, I am yearning to be free, and when I am, Ragnarok will begin."

"Be patient, my child. The moon will go dark in three days. That is when your bonds will break and you will once again be free to roam. Charlotte's powers won't develop that quickly. So a few more days is all you will have to wait."

"When I am free, I will wreak darkness on mankind and take my rightful position among the immortals. My enemies will bow before me, but I will show them no mercy."

"Yes, my son. There will be no mercy."

# # #

The next day, Charlotte was arranging the books on one of the shelves when Arnold Hunt startled her. "I didn't hear you come in," she said embarrassed. "I get so caught up in these books that I..."

"I'm sorry I surprised you," he apologized. "That was a nice tune you were humming. It was different than the last one I heard."

He moved next to her and ran a hand along the tops of the books she had arranged. "I don't know much about music, but the books appear to be arranged approximating the notes on a musical staff. Do you position them that way on purpose?"

"I never noticed that before," she said, running a finger along the same path that his hand had travelled. She hummed the tune again. "Interesting," she said.

Turning to face him. "You came back, Mr. Hunt."

"Please, call me Arnie. I wanted to let you know that I found the book I was looking for so you don't waste your time trying to find it here."

She blushed. "Is there another reason you came to see me?"

He blushed. "I'd like to be friends with you, and wanted to know if you take lunch breaks? We could meet later at the café down the street."

"I'd like that too…, Arnie," she said, looking into his steel-blue eyes. "I'll close the shop at twelve thirty and meet you there."

"Wonderful. See you then."

When he departed, her attention returned to the row of books he pointed out and she hummed again.

That evening, Aunt Unni finished sprinkling the bread with a light brown powder and squeezing a few colorless drops of liquid into a milk glass before her niece entered the kitchen.

"May I help you with anything, auntie?"

"Yes dear. Take the milk and bread and put them on the table; I will bring the meat. Everything else is already waiting for us."

Soon, Charlotte was joined at the table by her aunt. When seated, the girl took a sip from her milk glass, then casually said, "That school teacher came back to the shop today."

"Oh? That's twice this week, isn't it?" Unni nonchalantly answered.

"We had lunch together."

Her aunt stared at her niece. "You didn't eat the lunch I prepared for you?"

"Not today."

"But I *always* make your lunch, dear. That way I know you're getting good foods. You never know what is in the food you eat from somewhere else and especially restaurant food."

"Don't worry, auntie. I barely ate a thing. I was too caught up in the conversation we were having."

"What could you two have to talk about?"

"He made me aware that I was arranging books in a musical fashion and then subconsciously hummed the notes. Then, he told me about how music and mathematics seem to be so closely related. Did you know that there is a correlation between time travel and mathematics? He was so fascinating, auntie. He also told me there was a total lunar eclipse coming in a few nights. We discussed that for a while as I have been having dreams about the moon."

Her aunt shifted uncomfortably in her chair trying to be disinterested in the topic of their conversation. "You never told me his name, dear?"

"Arnold Hunt. But he comes from Scandinavian roots, like we do."

"And how do you know that?" she gingerly asked.

"His birth name was Arnbjorg, but he changed it to Arnold."

Suddenly, her aunt gasped, as though she were struggling for breath.

Charlotte moved quickly to her. "Are you alright, auntie? What can I do?"

After a few seconds, her aunt waved her off, and breathing again said, "I'll be okay. A piece of meat lodged in my throat, but I managed to swallow it. Whew, that was a scary moment."

"It was something I said that made you gasp, auntie. I could tell," Charlotte insisted. "What was it?"

"Arnbjorg. The name Arnbjorg took me by surprise."

Puzzled, the girl retook her seat. "Why would that name startle you so, auntie?"

Unni had to think of something fast. She stuttered as she came up with a story.

"Arnbjorg was the name of the man that was involved with your parent's death. You were so little when it happened. I've tried to keep the details from you, and I'm still not willing to share them. Perhaps another day I'll tell you. But for now, do an old woman an indulgence and stay home a few days. I am fearful that our family is being revisited by the past. I don't want you to come into contact with that man until I have time to think about it."

"But I can't just stay away. Who will run the bookstore?"

"I'll call the owner," Unni answered. "He will understand. Please, just two days is all I am asking. Then I'll tell you everything."

Charlotte reluctantly agreed to stay home, but only with the condition that her aunt promise to explain everything to her.

"Eat your bread, dear. You must be starved."

Taking the coffer from the closet, Aunt Unni placed it on her dresser and spoke. "Arnbjorg is here, my son. The girl has met him."

"Release me *NOW*, mother!" said a gravelly voice. "I will slay Arnbjorg just as I intend to slay the others."

"We must wait two more days, Fenrir. Then, you will be strong enough. If the girl and Arnbjorg were to combine their strengths now, I am afraid you will forever be bound to the darkness."

A guttural growl showed impatience. "And what if he comes here before then? You will have no choice but to release me. I will devour him as I devoured the hand of Tyr, son of Odin!"

"Patience, my son. I have asked her to stay away from the place they meet, but just in case, I have given her a stronger potion. It will keep her sleepy. We only have two more nights to wait. That is a blink of the eye in eternity. Rest now and gather your strength for Ragnarok. I will come for you when it is time."

She placed the coffer in its place on the shelf of her closet and went about her preparations.

The day of the total eclipse...

Aunt Unni entered Charlotte's bedroom in the afternoon carrying a bed tray of food. She set it upon a small table, then tried to arouse her niece. Shaking her, she said, "Wake up little one... you must eat."

Charlotte stirred, then rolled over onto her back. Slowly she came out of her stupor and tried to focus on her aunt's wrinkled face. "Where am I? What day is it?"

"It is a glorious day today," her aunt responded with enthusiasm. "You must eat, so that you are strong. I have some bread and porridge for you, my dear."

Charlotte yawned and attempted to sit while saying, "I'm not hungry right now, auntie. Leave the tray, and I will try to eat in a while."

"Alright my dear. But I must go out for a brief period. I will check on you when I return. I promise not to be away long."

Charlotte gave a faint wave, snuggled into the covers, and fell back asleep.

Unni patted her on the back and departing the room, she uttered, "It is a glorious day indeed."

A short while later, Charlotte was aroused from her deep sleep by sounds coming from the room next to hers. She caught sight of the bed tray and reached for a piece of bread and brought it to her mouth. But before eating, an odd sensation embraced her, so she returned the bread to the tray.

Suddenly, the noise in the next room grew more disturbing. She forced herself out of bed and into the hall. Still feeling the effects of deep sleep, she placed her hand on her aunt's bedroom door to steady herself and called out to Unni. "Auntie… auntie, are you alright?"

She heard a low growl, and tried the door handle. It opened.

A guttural, *"Let me out of here!"* came from inside the closet.

Still in a stupor, she envisioned her aunt stuck inside the closet and opened the door. But her aunt was not there.

The voice sounded again, only slightly more pleasant this time but still with a growl. "Little one, let me out!"

The sound was coming from a box above her head. She reached up, teetering slightly, and pulled it from the shelf. Holding the box, she imagined a monstrous wolf standing in front of a darkened moon. A shiver ran down her spine taking some of the sleepiness from her.

"What are you doing? screeched Unni, grabbing the box from her niece.

"I-I heard a voice calling out to me. It came from inside that box," she stated, pointing to it.

"*Nonsense! You were dreaming,*" Unni said with irritation in her voice. Then ordered, "*Go to your room, I will be there in a minute.*"

When the girl exited the room, Unni scolded. "*I told you it is not time, Fenrir. You only have a few more hours to wait!*"

Outside the bedroom, Charlotte had stayed to listen through the crack in the door.

The strange voice continued, "I am tired of waiting, mother! *I want out now*! Just lift the lid, so that I can breathe in this world."

Unni answered, "The timing has to be perfect, my son. Otherwise you will not have the power to defeat the Norse Gods. And you do want your revenge, don't you? Be still, my son, the hour approaches fast when the rooster crows to the Gods and heroes at Valhalla warning them that Ragnarok has begun."

Unni then heard a creak on a floorboard outside her room. She hurriedly placed the box back on the shelf. While shoving it back against a pile of sweaters, a corner of the box lifted slightly. She closed the closet door and went to attend to her niece.

Entering her niece's room, she saw Charlotte sitting on the edge of the bed with an empty porridge bowl in her hand. Unni's demeanor softened. "I'm sorry I yelled at you, Charlotte. I got worried when I returned and didn't find you in your room. You are in no condition to be walking around yet. I am glad that you ate something. How about some bread, dear?" she offered, holding the plate.

"I'm quite full now, auntie." Charlotte yawned. "I'll try and join you later for dinner. I think I'm going to rest some more, if that is all right with you?" Charlotte laid under the covers and rolled to her side.

Unni picked up the tray and eyeing the empty bowl said, "Yes, dear. Rest. I'll leave you to sleep." She then quietly departed.

After only a few minutes, Charlotte got out of bed and dressed. She realized she had to get away from the house. A sense was telling her that evil was about to descend on the world, and that her aunt was part of her feeling. But where would she go? Then, a single thought crossed her mind and she softly spoke in reaction, "Arnie!"

Being careful not to make a sound, Charlotte heard her aunt busy in the kitchen as her foot hit the last step. Relieved, she grabbed a sweater and silently let herself out the front door.

#

Meanwhile, in the darkness of Unni's wardrobe, the partially ajar box lid started to tremble.

#

Arnold Hunt was surprised to see Charlotte waiting for him outside the middle school.

"This is a nice surprise. I came by the bookstore yesterday to see you, but it was closed."

It was then he saw she was in distress. "What is it?" he said, placing his hands on her arms.

"I can't explain it, but something terrible is about to happen. You must believe me. We must go to the bookstore."

She looked to the sky as the first sight of the rising moon began to appear at the horizon. Come!" she ordered, and pulled him in that direction.

When they reached their destination, she locked the door behind them, moved to a row of books on a shelf above her head, and started to hum according to the pattern they made.

Bewildered, Arnie asked again. "What is it, Charlotte? What is going on?"

Over her shoulder, she replied, "I had a vision of a great, monstrous wolf howling before a dark moon and it signaled the end of time as we know it. I know it doesn't make sense, but you and I are the only ones that can stop it."

"That tune you're humming… it is familiar to me, but I don't know why."

"Norse mythology refers to it as a lokk – the singing of messages and signals. It starts with a long note, which then drops to a lower note. This is followed by some short cries, which may in turn, be followed by the calling of the names of animals."

"You mean a cow or something?" he asked.

"*That's it Arnie*! I saw a stag on a carved coffer in my aunt's closet. I heard a voice call to me to let whatever was inside loose. My aunt grabbed it from me and inferred it was my imagination. I feel she has been keeping something terrible from me. I also have a sense she has been tampering with my food... as if she used a magic potion on me. I threw out some porridge she made for me so she would think I ate it. But there is more..."

"I don't understand why, but I believe you," he said. "Remember my telling you there is a correlation between time travel and mathematics?" he asked.

She nodded affirmatively.

"In the book I was looking for when we first met, I read a theory that musical notes and mathematics are intertwined and the right combination can alter time. You said a lokk starts with a long note, but the books on the shelf you are looking at has a short book among the taller ones at the beginning. Maybe if we rearrange the sequence..."

"Yes, take that book," she said excitedly, pointing to the one he inferred. "I'm having a vision of page eighty-two."

He removed the book and saw that it was a book of Norse mythology. Turning to page eighty-two he read aloud: *Eikthyrnir is a stag that stands on the roof of Valhalla. When, the monstrous wolf, Fenrir, escapes his bonds the stag bounds off to warn of Ragnarok. The first to see the wolf will be a valkyrie named Brynhildr who is a shield maiden condemned by Odin to live the life of a mortal. To redeem herself, she will call upon Arnbjorg, who fights the great wolf until Odin's son Vidar rides his father's eight-legged horse from Valhalla and kills the great wolf.*

Arnie looked at Charlotte. "Your visions... can you be Brynhildr?"

She equally returned his startled look. "And you're Arnbjorg!"

"This is crazy!" he said. "I'm not a superhero!"

"Not in human form," she replied, "but some force brought us together."

He looked into her green eyes. "I believe your humming the notes can alter time, but what will happen, I don't know."

Aunt Unni heard a terrible sound coming from upstairs. She feared the worse and waited. It wasn't long before a loud roar shook the house and a giant wolf's head poked through the kitchen door where Unni was standing.

"*Free at last!*" growled the beast loudly. "Ragnarok has begun. But before I destroy Odin, I will slay the girl, Brynhildr, and then Arnbjorg."

"I told you to wait!" Unni shouted. "It is not time. You will not have the power of the dark moon with you."

"My bonds have been broken; there is nothing to stop me now. And once I take out those mortals, then I shall wreak my vengeance on all of Valhalla."

The giant wolf turned, crashed out the front door, and followed the scent of his prey to the bookstore. Upon arriving there, he pawed at the door and roared, "*I have come to feast and let this world know that Fenrir is alive!*"

"We must hurry," said Charlotte, pushing aside some books on the shelf. "Place the book here," she said to Arnie. "The beast is here and I must signal for Vidar."

As soon as the book was positioned in the space she indicated, Charlotte began to hum according to the pattern of the books.

When Fenrir heard her tune, he roared, *"Go ahead Brynhildr, signal for Vidar. But before he arrives, you will be but an aftertaste."* He then threw his full weight against the door, but it held against his first assault.

The humming grew louder. Her rhythm first steady then dropping to a lower tone as indicated by the position of the books. Then she wailed and cried out the name of Eikthyrnir.

The earth trembled under their feet and suddenly, Charlotte and Arnie were transformed into the immortals they truly were.

The wolf crashed through the door - his huge body practically filled the room and saliva dripped from his colossal teeth. He sneered at the two standing before him and in his raspy voice growled, "You are no match for me. I am unfettered now and you heroes will be my first victims."

Arnie swept an arm across Charlotte pushing her behind him. "You will have to go through me first," he bravely said.

There was a pause. "I know you, Arnbjorg," said the monstrosity. "You are the eagle and protector. And strong you may be, but I am stronger, and on this day I bring doom to all the heroes of Valhalla, so maybe it is fitting I start with you."

Then he snapped his massive jaws at Arnbjorg.

"Brynhildr, you know what to do," Arnie said, then lunged at the great wolf grabbing the upper and lower jaws of the beast - one in each hand. His arms, now massive, keeping the sharp teeth from grinding into his flesh and bones. As if one being, they clashed and wrestled and fell out into the pale light of the rising moon.

Charlotte stepped back as the two fought. She again hummed her melodious tune, wailed, and cried out to Eikthyrnir.

With the moon ascending, the first shadow of darkness began to cross it. Arnbjorg's arms were weakening against the force of the wolf, and the jaws of the beast began to close ever so slightly. *"Brynhildr, I can't last much longer. Run and save yourself,"* he implored.

Suddenly, there was a brilliant flash of light and the Norse God, Vidar, appeared. He descended from the sky, riding a gray, eight-legged horse, toward the ensuing battle below.

Alighting next to the beast, he drew his sword. It gleamed in the light of the moon. Then he thrust it deep into the heart of the great wolf.

Writhing, the strength of the monstrous wolf began to fade. Arnbjorg held his grip until the very last movement of the beast was stilled.

Vidar went to Brynhildr. "Odin condemned you to live the life of a mortal woman after your treachery, but for saving Valhalla from Fenrir, he has offered you to return as valkyrie and live as an immortal."

She looked into his eyes, and then the steel-blue eyes of Arnbjorg knowing she had to make a decision.

#

The next morning, Charlotte awoke and rolled toward her husband. "Arnie, I just had the strangest dream."

END

Author's Note

Thank you for reading my book! I would love to hear from you. You can email me through my website http://www.anthony-mays.com

I certainly hope you had as much fun reading my book as I had writing it. If you liked it, please tell a friend, or better yet, tell the world by writing a review on Amazon. Even a few short sentences are helpful. As an independently published author, I don't have a marketing department behind me. I have you, the reader. So please spread the word!

Thanks again, and all my best,
Anthony Mays

About the Author

Anthony was born and raised west of Philadelphia, Pennsylvania. He went into military service at the age of seventeen and retired after serving twenty years. Anthony subsequently received his Bachelor's degree from the University of Nebraska at Omaha. Too young to stop working, he made a second career as a civil servant in the U.S. government, enjoying positions for both the Internal Revenue Service and the Department of Veterans Affairs. Along with his wife Sherry, he enjoys sharing the experiences of their three children, their significant others, and four blessed grandchildren. Most vacations are spent near water where Anthony envisions finding the next great treasure trove. In the meantime, he is excited to take pieces of his life experiences and mold them into fictional works of art.

Novels by Anthony Mays
Halfway to a Southern Heart
http://amazon.com/dp/B00PO6ZTII

Halfway to Uncertainty
http://amazon.com/dp/B00PNV0AMO

Halfway to the Truth   http://amazon.com/dp/B00XJQVJ7A

Halfway to Magnolia House
http://amazon.com/dp/B01AML01O6

Made in the USA
Middletown, DE
09 July 2016